The Second Hand Wife

Rajesh Ku. Sharma
M.Sc., MFA.

BLUEROSE PUBLISHERS
India | U.K.

Copyright © R. K. Sharma 2025

All rights reserved by author. No part of this publication may be reproduced, stored in a retrieval system or transmitted in any form or by any means, electronic, mechanical, photocopying, recording or otherwise, without the prior permission of the author. Although every precaution has been taken to verify the accuracy of the information contained herein, the publisher assumes no responsibility for any errors or omissions. No liability is assumed for damages that may result from the use of information contained within.

BlueRose Publishers takes no responsibility for any damages, losses, or liabilities that may arise from the use or misuse of the information, products, or services provided in this publication.

For permissions requests or inquiries regarding this publication, please contact:

BLUEROSE PUBLISHERS
www.BlueRoseONE.com
info@bluerosepublishers.com
+91 8882 898 898
+4407342408967

ISBN: 978-93-6783-075-8

First Edition: February 2025

Introduction

This book is the output of 40 years of experience in my life. Whatever I have seen and observed that I have written in this book. This is my second book. I have already published my one book.

In this book I have mentioned the characteristics of some of the ladies and gents who had more than one affair or spouse. Some of the people have affairs with someone else and they marry someone else.

Some of the people have post marital affairs. It will destroy the piece of your mind and your family.

In many countries such kinds of people are available. In some of the stories they were forced to do so and in others they did it willingly for their enjoyment. In some of the stories I have written about molestation and damaging modesty of girls. Please note down If anyone is damaging the modesty of girls then she will never forgive you and you will never be happy because of her cursing words. When one spouse is enough for all their needs then why did they go for the second?

You cannot be happy all the time. You will always be busy thinking that she was better but whatever God has given you that is the best one and please be happy with that.

Sex is not so important. It will give you pleasure for a few minutes only. Only sex is not life.

It will not give you name and fame. It will not give you wealth and prestige in your society.

There are lots of things in the world which are more important. Some of the works are there which really need our attention but we ignore them because we are selfish.

All the time having sex in mind will disturb your mental peace. It will pressurize you all the time to think about it. Somewhere you will be in economic loss also due to this.

And if you are in student life then certainly it will disturb your studies.

We should have some great personalities as our role models and try to follow them. We should try to adopt their hard work and goodness. We should engage ourselves in some productive and proud work.

God will always do well for you. God has kept something better for you.

Thank you.
R.K. Sharma
Editor

Index.   Page no.

1. The Real Love   1
2. The Roadside Home   4
3. The Robbers   7
4. The Room Partner   10
5. She Ran Away   15
6. The Mistake   19
7. The Partner   22
8. The Boyfriend   25
9. Betrayed   28
10. Hope Mine   31
11. Power   34
12. Misfortune   38
13. Greedy People   41
14. Trapped   44
15. A Courageous lady   47
16. Hanged his wife   51
17. The Nurse   55
18. The Marriage   57
19. The Love Birds   59
20. A Fake Love   63
21. A Plot   65
22. The love on the roof   67
23. Friendship   70
24. A Blind Love   72
25. Two Friends   75
26. The Twins   80
27. She Sold Herself   83
28. Accident   85
29. The Dream Came True   87
30. Miss Beauty   89

31. Love In The Village	91
32. Love In The Cropping Fields	94
33. Boyfriends	97
34. The Selfish Girl	101
35. The Hotel Party	103
36. The Dirty Uncle	105
37. The Clever Girl	110
38. A Night In Calcutta	112
39. The Small Hotels	114
40. Mr Idiot	116
41. Struggle	120
42. The Petrol Pump Manager	124
43. The Sale	127
44. Shamelessness	129
45. A Love Marriage Family	130
46. The Judgment	133
47. A Placement Agency	137

1. The Real love

This is the story of Haryana. When I completed my graduation and moved to Delhi NCR to find a job in any multinational company as a management trainee. I was staying in Gurgaon. In my neighbourhood one Bengali family was living. There were only three members in that family: mother , daughter and a son. Mother was older in age. Her son was starting in class 4 only in a government school. Their daughter was named Ishita. She was an undergraduate. She had stopped her studies and was trying to find a job in any of the companies.

When Ishita saw me, she liked me and tried to have an affair with me. But I didn't like it and didn't see her . I completely ignored it. There was a boy named Brendon who liked her a lot. Brendon was also residing with my neighbourhood. Ishita did not like Brendon because he was from a poor family. Brendon has stopped his study after class tenth because of poverty. He was not having enough money for higher studies so he also started looking for any kind of job in any of the companies.

Brendon told me that loves Ishita. I said ok , you can continue with her.

He replied - but she did not like me. I asked him how he knew that. He told me when I was going to meet her she poured water on me and she tease me also. I asked him have you seen her pouring water on any of the strangers. I also asked have you seen her teasing any other person in the neighbourhood. Brendon said no. I said this is real love. She wants to play with you. She wants to have fun with you. That's why she has poured water on you and she was teasing you. She loves you by heart which She was also not knowing. This is real love. Brendon said ok. I also did not understand her true love. Today onwards I will also enjoy this kind of fun. Brendon asked then why she directly proposed to me. I said because you are not having any job. Brendon said ok. Today onwards I will never sit home. I am going to find a job.

Ishita was also looking for a job. She has applied in many of the companies so she has got a job in a newly established company. Ishita Started going for work every day in the morning and coming back in the evening. Ishita has stopped looking here and there because she was not having enough time for these things now. Ishita was in her teenage years and she was also deprived of having a boyfriend. She started an affair with her boss in the company and continues. One day Ishita came with her boss to her rented flat. She locked her flat from inside with her boss and her mother and brother were sitting outside of the flat. All her neighbours saw this and came to know her misdeeds birthday did not speak anything because her mother was also sitting there.

When Brendon came to know all these things he became very upset. He told me about this. I said it happened only because you are not having a job. Ishita started an affair with her boss because he is a earning person. Brendon was depressed. I sympathize with him. After a few days Brendon also got a job. He asked me also to see his company and took me along with him for that. He got a job as a helper in a garment industry. He was very happy. I congratulated him for his new job. Brendon became very busy. He was also going in the morning and coming back in the evening till 7 o'clock. But he did not forget Ishita. He announces to his family that he will be married to Ishita only. His parents try to make him understand that she is of a different religion and we are from different religions so it is not possible. Brendon said she is a girl and I am a boy. It is enough for our marriage. I don't believe in caste and religion. Brandon's parents said she will be a second hand bike for you and what about her affair with her boss. Brendon said it is an old story I have forgotten. You should also forget it.

Brendon said Ishita had promised me that she will never have any affair with anyone. It is enough for me and she is my childhood love so I cannot forget her. Brendon's parents became ready for his marriage with Ishita under the pressure of his son. It was a love cum arranged marriage. This is the real love Brendon has got married with his childhood love. Lots of congratulations to them. He has two children now.

****

2. The Road Side Home

Every day I was walking to school from a highway. Roadside area was full of buildings. Many people were living there. At that time my age was 16 years. There was a very beautiful teenage girl in one of the buildings whose name was Pinky. She was always standing on the gate of her roadside house whenever I saw. She was very beautiful just like a beauty queen. She was lean and thin. Her height was approx 5 foot 4 inches. She was so attractive that no one can pass from there without seeing her. She was very charming, her eyes, nose, ears, cheeks, chin, and her hairstyle were as beautiful as a fairy's face. It seemed that God had given enough time during her creation. Her father was not alive and her brothers were working in other states for livelihood because her family was very poor. She was staying there with her mother only. She was not going to school or college because of her poverty.

She was not having any other work to do so she was standing on her gate all the time looking for a nice boyfriend. I was also having some kind of affection for her. She offered her friendship to a smart person named Jimmy and he accepted it. She did not know that the person she had selected for her friendship was rowdy in that area. For two or three days Pinky and her new boyfriend became busy gossiping. When Pinky trusted him she started calling him in her house during the day hour and gossiping a lot. Her mother did not object because he was calling her aunty and gossiping with her also sometimes. Her mother also trusted him.

After a few days Jimmy made a request to Pinky to call him at night for her love. Pinky trusted him and she was also hungry for his real love so she accepted his request. She said ok when my mother will be in the deep sleep you can come and I will open the door for you when you will call me at my gate. He came at night and Pinky opened her gate for him. Whole night they enjoyed their love together. In the early morning he went back. For a few days it continued and both of them were very happy.

One day Jimmy discussed these things with his friends. His friends asked him - do you want to marry that girl Pinky?

He clearly said no never.

It was earlier said that he was a rowdy person. His all the friends were also rowdies , they forced him to enjoy pinky's modesty with them and he also agreed under friends pressure. They planned that they all will go to Pinky's house today's night.

They did so. They all reached her house and Pinky's boyfriend Jimmy made a request to open the door. Pinky opened the door and they all entered forcibly. They took Pinky at gunpoint.

Pinky understood the whole matter. She started weeping stealthily and making lots of requests to her boyfriend to leave her house. She was telling her boyfriend - I want to marry you but what are you doing with me with your friends?

Please stop it. Please don't be betrayed. I am yours only and I will be your forever. Please stop your friends. He replied I am also on the gun so I cannot stop them. The all raped her one by one. Now it has become a routine affair for the rowdies. They started coming with their more friends every night and they all started molesting her. Every rowdy in that area enjoyed her modesty. In the whole area the messages spread that she is offering herself to everyone at night and every person of the area who wanted to enjoy with her they enjoyed. It continued for many years.

Now I was there in the nearby college. Like other people, I also came to know the whole story. One day I also got the message to enjoy with her. But I completely denied it and said I do not want to indulge in your bad activities.

Her brothers came back to home. They were working in other states. Her mother told everything to her brother. Her brother told that we cannot lodge an FIR because many people are there and after all we will be defamed. So it will be better to marry her with someone far from here.

They started looking for a groom. They fixed her marriage with someone of their community. She was married and moved to an in-laws house where she was safe now.

Roadside homes are very dangerous especially for those families who have young daughters at home.

****

3. The Robbers.

This is the story of a very nice colony. Many people were residing there happily. There was a family in which only three people were there. One elderly person who was going to work every day and coming late at night. His teenage son and a very beautiful adult girl Ruhi were there at home. Ruhi was their distant relative and came to live with them because of her poverty. Housewife of that family died a few years back due to some critical disease. The family came out from this trauma and were living happily. That family called Ruhi from her village to live with them so that their food for both the time she can prepare well. She was bored from her village so she became ready to come with them.

Ruhi was very happy with them because she was living in a nice colony and getting very nice food everyday which was not possible at her village.

I personally know that family very well because I was also living in the same colony. I was talking to everyone in the colony so many times I have gossiped with that family also.

Some thieves were also living in the nearby village. One day when those thieves were roaming in the colony they saw that elderly person coming late at home and they followed him. They saw his house. They observed from a distance - how he is coming, how the door was opened and who has opened the door? They also found out how many members are there in the family.

The thieves observed the same for a few days and made up a plan to rob their house. After a few days at night the thieves came fully prepared. They followed that elderly person at night and as soon as he called his family to open the door they all entered his house forcibly at gunpoint. The thieves tied them with rope, put tape on their mouths. They packed that elderly person and his son into the bathroom. They kept Ruhi with them at gunpoint and collected all the valuable items of their home. After that they all raped Ruhi one by one. Whole night they molested Ruhi. They didn't listen to her cry and pain. After that all the thieves left them and moved with all the items they robbed.

Ruhi was suffering with lots of pain but she managed to wake up and open the doors of the bathroom. She also cut the rope tied off by her family. After that she fell down in pain. That family understood the whole matter by seeing Ruhi in poor condition. They rushed to a doctor immediately. Ruhi was under treatment in the hospital. After a few hours the family came back to the home and left Ruhi in hospital for proper treatment.

They informed the Police station about the theft and called them. The police came and noted down their report. They saw that Police came without a dog squad and without forensic lab members. They also observed that Police are touching every item without using gloves. So they did not discuss the suffering of Ruhi and dropped the idea to lodge a case of molestation. They lodge and FIR of theft only. The police never came back to discuss any improvement about the case.

The FIR was totally wasted.

After a few days Ruhi got well. They brought her back home.

They decided to arrange a marriage ceremony for Ruhi as soon as possible because the incident took place only one week back.

Same year they found a very handsome groom for her and Ruhi was married Same year. I went to attend her marriage ceremony and saw the groom. He was really very handsome and smart just like a Hollywood hero. I met her husband a few years back. He is really a very smart and wealthy person. He has made a beautiful house. He had two very smart sons and Ruhi 's family was very happy now. It's very good that till date her husband does not know the story.

****

4. The Room Partner

I was residing in Delhi for study purposes. Delhi life was very interesting but very tough also. When we were living there we were thinking that it's a very tough life when we get off this life. It was very tough to manage food for both the times because if we cook then we will not get time for study purposes and if we are eating outside then the food is unhealthy and unhygienic. But anyhow we were managing it. Today when I am writing this story I am thinking that life was very very interesting. We cannot go back into that life because time never goes back.

we were living there for study purposes , we were in huge tension every day to get a job after study. But when I recall those days I personally become very happy remembering those days because I think that was the golden period of our life.

In Delhi rooms were very costly which was not affordable by middle class family students. So in the whole area of Delhi wherever students are living, they must have a room partner. It was a very big problem to find a good room partner. For that there was a big wall in our colony where all the students were pasting posters with detail to find a good room partner. Needful students were reading those posters and coming to the room to become a room partner. We were taking interviews with those students to make him our room partner. We were asking about their family background and economic status so that he is able to pay the room rent in advance every month and some other questions like whether he is vegetarian or non vegetarian etc. I have also faced the interview when I was finding a room for me in Delhi. But I passed that interview within 5 minutes and was shifted into the room the next day.

After a few years my room partner left that area so I was in need of a new room partner.

I also pasted a new poster on that Wall to find a room partner. Students started coming to my room to become my room partner and I was taking interviews with everyone. In maximum cases I denied them because they were non vegetarian. Finally a vegetarian student came and passed my interview and became my room partner. His name was Harry. He was a graduate and studying for a job. For a few months he studied well. After that he started wasting his time here and there.

One day he told me that his mausi is coming to Delhi for some kind of treatment. I did not think more and said ok you can go. Next day in the morning he came to my room with his very beautiful and young mausi named Lucie.

We were in student life and where we were studying we rarely saw any beautiful girls in those areas for many days. Today a very beautiful young girl was standing in my room. I was totally surprised and very happy to see her. Harry told me that in 2 - 3 hours they will become ready and go to the doctor. I said okay. They were getting ready, so I brought some snacks and fruits for them to eat and move for the treatment. For those hours my study was completely disturbed. When they went out again my study was disturbed because I was thinking about the beauty of his mausi Lucie. Whole day was lost and in the evening Harry again came with Lucie. In the evening I brought some food items and we enjoyed dinner together. After that in the late evening Harry told me to go to sleep with my another friend in the same locality because only two beds were there where he and his mausi Lucie would sleep. I said okay and went out to sleep somewhere else. In the morning I came back and knocked on the door. They were still sleeping. I told please wake up, you have to go to visit a doctor. They wake up, open the door and get ready to visit a doctor. Harry was not happy because I disturbed their sleeping. Lucie was looking very healthy, fit and fine. I don't know what kind of treatment she was taking. I never asked Harry and he also did not discuss it with me. They took their breakfast and left the room. In the evening they came back. I told Harry that today I am unable to go to sleep somewhere else because my friend is not there. He has gone somewhere.

He said okay. Harry went out with Lucy and came back again after having dinner. I asked Harry how we will sleep together in one room because only two beds were there, one for me and one for my room partner Harry. He replied that on one bed you will sleep on another bef Lucy will sleep and he will sleep on the floor. I was not happy with this arrangement but there was no way so we agreed. We did so but then I woke up in the morning I saw that Harry was sleeping with Lucie in the same bed. I asked Harry about this then he told me in the morning he was feeling very cold so did this. Harry also said treatment is completed so Lucie is going back to her village. I did not think more and said OK. Lucie was going back and Harry left her up at the railway station.

We continued our study as earlier. After one month Harry again told Lucie is coming for treatment again. I asked Harry if he was told the treatment is over then he replied - doctor has given appointment for this month. I asked about the disease and he told me these are ladies' problems. I didn't ask for more. Harry brought Lucie in the morning and went out with her for treatment after having breakfast.

After two three hours a person came in search of Harry and Lucie. I asked who are you? He replied he is the mamaji of Harry and brother of Lucie. I told him that Harry had gone with Lucie for the treatment to a doctor. He asked what the problem was and I told I don't know but last month they also went for the treatment. He asked for the address of the doctor or hospital. I said he did not discuss this with me. He said that Lucie is also living in North Delhi and for maximum time she is not available at her rented room. He said next month Lucie's marriage ceremony is fixed with someone and she is wasting her time with Harry. He was having doubts about the relationship between Harry and Lucie. He asked - can I wait here for their returning after treatment. I said why not you are the relative of Harry and Lucie both.

In the evening when Harry returned with Lucie at the room and they saw Mamaji sitting and waiting for them their faces were totally blank. Firstly mamaji slapped Lucy very tightly and took her with him to the village. As soon as Harry saw that Mama Ji had slapped Lucie he ran away with full speed from there.

I also noticed that Harry was leaving the room at 9 o'clock in the morning after taking breakfast and coming back till 8 o'clock in the evening. Which doctor or hospital was giving this much time for her treatment. I don't know if they were going for a treatment or Delhi tourism.

Harry did not return for one week. After that he came back, gave me the room rent and vacated the room without discussing anything with me because his love affair was over. We all knew his secret now . He was feeling very ashamed so did not discuss anything and went forever. Lucie was now the second hand wife of her husband. He will never know.

****

5. She Ran Away

This is the story of a village girl named Alisha. When Alisha was born her parents were worried about her health because she was very weak. But later on her health improved. She was the third child of their parents and the other two were her elder brothers. The family was a lower middle class family. Her village was very famous for sweets and wrestlers. I have personally visited that village many times. Children grow day by day. Alisa was now in class 10th but she was having an affair with a boy named Raj of her class. Both of them were in love for the last 2 years. During Holi Raj was coming to her house and pouring her colour from a window. Alisha was very happy with him. Alisa was going to school every day only to meet him. During Diwali Raj was cracking crackers in front of her door then Alisha's father was thinking that some rowdies are disturbing them so started shouting and warning all those children who were cracking crackers but Raj ran away before that. Many times it happened during Diwali. Alisha was happy, she was enjoying these things. Alisha and Raj both of them appeared in class 10th board examinations after that they were free from study for a few months. Now Alisa was at her home. She was not able to meet Raj for a single minute during the day.

So Alisha made a plan with Raj on a phone call that they will move to the next city and get married. In starting Raj denied but agreed to inner planning. They planned that the next day they will leave their house by giving the excuse to their families that they are having practice in the school and they will run away together from the village. They did the same as per their planning. Alisa was having some clothes in her bag. Raj had many items in his bag.

After school time when Alisha did not return home, parents started searching here and there in the village and area near by this school. Alisha's Father reached to school and asked the school guard about them. The school guard told him that school was closed. It was not open today. Alisha's father was shocked. He understood that Alisa had left the village with her lover. He was having doubts about Raj so he moved to his house. He called the parents of Raj. Raj was not available in the village and his phone was also switched off. Alisha's father started beating the parents of Raj and told them that their son had kidnapped Alisha.

Alisha's father moved to the police station with some of the villagers and lodged an FIR against Raj and his friends. Police officer was also asking lots of questions and they were telling him that it might be possible that your daughter had run away with her boyfriend. It is common for girls and boys of adolescent age. The police officer lodged an FIR and gave him a copy of the FIR.

Alisha's father sent the copy of the FIR to all the newspapers and media persons. So that if Alisha and Raj will read the newspaper they will know that the Police are also in search of them.

Alisha's father was in deep distress because his daughter was missing. Her mother and whole family members were also in deep distress. Whole day her family was crying.

They made calls to all the distant relatives to find out Alisha was kidnapped. He told all the villagers also that Alisa was kidnapped by someone. All villages and family members were searching for Alisha on different railway stations and bus stands.

For three days Alisha did not return home. Her family members were suffering with the fear of defaming in the village and among their relatives.

On the 3rd day one of the relatives informed them that Alisha is visible in Calcutta. He informed all his relatives residing in Calcutta to hold them from the railway station. His relatives did the same. They catch Alisa and Raj together. Alisha's father and other relatives moved to Calcutta immediately by a private car and arrived within a few hours. They meet Alisha and Raj both. They slapped Raj very tightly and handed him over to the nearest police station by showing the copy of the FIR. Raj was making lots of request to the police that he has not kidnapped Alisha, she has run away with him willingly by herself. They were in love. He is a lover not a kidnapper. Raj said to the police that if he would kidnap Alisha then how her old dresses would be there in his bag. The police officer did not listen and arrested Raj and kept him in captivity on the basis of an FIR lodged against him.

The police officer formed the next police station where an FIR was lodged.

Alisha's family brought her back home. Next day in the morning Alisa was also supposed to report in the police station and to give her statement in front of the police officers and the court. Alisha's family counselled her to give the statement against Raj. Alisha did the same. She complained against Raj. Raj was sent to Jail on the charge of kidnapping.

Alisha's family left the village forever and as soon as Alisha crossed the age of 18 years they fixed her marriage ceremony with someone. Alisha was a married lady now. She was a second hand wife, but her husband never knew it, because she never visited the village.

****

6. Mistake

Amit was a very young staff member in a reputed office which had more than hundred branches all over the world. He was very energetic and a good sports person also. He was ready to work for everyone so all the office staff were very happy with him. He never said no for any kind of work in his office. After a few days a new young female staff member Sheela joined the office. Sheela was young and unmarried so Amit was attracted towards her from the very first day. They were working together and started helping each other in all the work. Sheela was impressed with his work. Amit and Sheela started playing badminton with other office staff during their free time. They started consuming lunch together and now they were sharing with each other all the edible items. Both of them were consuming water with the same glass without cleaning it. Everything was clearly visible to all the staffs but they didn't interrupt.

Sheela started meeting with Amit in the evening at different shopping malls, mega marts, hotels and restaurants etc . Their love affair was growing day by day but whenever Sheela asked Amit to go to his rented flat Amit completely denied it because Amit was a fraud. He was having an affair with one more girl who was always coming to his flat. His previous girlfriend was living just near his flat so he was unable to greet Sheela in his flat.

Amit and Sheela both started coming to the office and going back from the office on the same bike which was pinching to all the staff because they were not sitting properly on the bike. They were touching each other on the bike in a bad manner which was not good for a civilized person. One day when Sheela forced Amit to go to his flat, Amit told that renovation work is going on there so next week maybe he will invite Sheela to his flat.

Sheela said OK.

Amit broke up with his previous girlfriend. His previous girlfriend fought badly with him and took away his costly belongings and educational certificates with her and refused to return it in spite of making lots of requests because many times Amit has had intercourse with her. Amit was in a big problem because his educational certificates were there with his previous girlfriend. He discussed all these problems with his fast friends. His friends played a vital role as mediator between Amit and his previous girlfriend. They counseled her and promised to fulfill her one demand in lieu of returning his certificates, then she became ready and returned his certificates. The matter with his previous girlfriend was over now.

Amit changed his flat and invited Sheela there. Sheela became very happy after seeing his flat. Everyday after dispersal from the office Amit and Sheela started spending time in the flat and many times they also had intercourse also. Sheela was willing to marry Amit but he denied many times by giving some reasons. Amit was enjoying her modesty, he was not in any mood to marry her because he was a fraud. He was betraying her which she didn't realize.

After 2 years Amit got a new job in a government office in another City which he joined and broke up with Sheela. He stopped receiving her phone calls also. Sheela was in deep distress now but unable to do anything. She was repenting of her mistake of making an affair with Amit and she cried a lot. She forgot her relationship with Amit.

Sheela was going to be married to someone else. She was not ready but agreed under parental pressure. She was a second hand wife for someone.

****

7. The Partner

Salma was a new employee in a government office. She joined as a regular employee there. She was unmarried, beautiful and a postgraduate employee. When she came for duty on the first day by chance she met me because I was standing there for some kind of work . She asked me about duty and whom to report. I guided her. From the next day she started coming and continued to come on duty regularly. We all were working together as usual. Whenever she had any problem related to office administration she discussed it with me and I helped her as much as possible.

One day she was willing to celebrate her birthday among all the staff members. She asked her colleagues for help and they did so. She asked me also, I helped her then she became very impressed with me. She was discussing all her problems related to duty and home with me.

One day someone made a scratch mark on her new car intentionally to disturb her, which made her very annoyed and unhappy. People residing near her flat were not helpful. They were jealous of her because an unmarried girl was residing alone in their locality and earning a lot. Whenever she was in need of help she came to me and I helped her. She was attracted to me, I was unaware of this, I never thought from that side because I am a married person. I think she did not know that I was married. She bought a two BHK flat in the next locality from my colony. She also bought a new car. One day when we were gossiping in the office area during free time she made a request to me to find a room partner for her because she was not feeling well living alone in that apartment. She was in need of a friend for goshipping in her flat also. She discussed the rent. I said OK I will try to find a lady to reside with you. I was totally unaware that indirectly she was asking me to become her room partner.

After a few days I heard that she has kept a male room partner from our office named Akbar. I know Akbar personally. He was not a good person but I did not have any proof to prove that he is not good. But Akbar was room partner of Salma. She kept a male room partner because she was in need of something else. They were in a living relationship for 3 months without informing their parents. Everyday Salma and Akbar were coming to duty together in Salma's car. It continued for 3 months. After that Salma started treating Akbar as her servant. He was carrying her bag and other belongings wherever she was moving, even to the duty place. Every staff member on duty came to know about their relationship. Some of Akbar's friends started teasing him that he had become her servant. Akbar felt it was very bad. Akbar vacated her flat after pinching comments from his friends but he has enjoyed her flat and many more things for 3 months.

Salma's marriage was fixed with an army personnel. She informed all her friends but none of the staff members or colleagues.

But she invited me through phone calls. She made a request to me to send my housemaid for the household work for 7 days or till her marriage ceremony is going to be completed. I said okay I'll send. Next day I sent one maid to her flat. She worked well till the completion of her marriage ceremony.

Salma was a married lady now but she was a second hand wife. Within a year she gave birth to a new baby. She resigned from the duty and left the station for ever. She sent her resignation letter by email.

****

8. The Boyfriend

Prema was a good girl by nature. She was good at studying. She was short heighted. Prema's whole family was short heighted.

Prema was a very dark complexioned girl. No one liked her in her childhood except her parents. It was because of her colour and dull face. In her school life when she became adolescent her friends were discussing their boyfriends but she was not. she was having any because of her dull face and colour. In her college life every friend had a boyfriend except Prema. Prema was very unhappy due to this reason because whomever she liked they did not even like to see her well.

Sometimes she was very very unhappy but not able to discuss this reason with her family. She was understanding the reason by herself.

She has completed her post graduate degree and she took an education degree also. Now her college life is over and she has joined a reputed public school as a PGT.

Her school was very far from her house so she needed a rented house. For this she discusses in her class 11 with the students. One of the students, David, said that he will find a rented house for her within a week.

Next day David told Prema that he had seen a rented house for her just near his home. Prema madam asked to show that house. David told ok madam after dispersal of the school you can come with me I will show you that house. She became ready to go with him.

Prema went to see that home and liked it because it was cheaper in rate compared to other localities. Prema shifted into that house and started coming to school every day from there only.

David started liking her. Because he was a student of adolescence. Students of this age are always in search of someone whom they can love and enjoy. Generally they do not see the age and beauty in front of hunger of love. Prema also started liking. Prema was deprived of having a boyfriend for a long time. It was going to fulfill her long awaited wish. It doesn't matter if he was her student and very younger than her.

Prema was feeling very lucky that she has got a very young, smart and energetic boyfriend.

Without parents' permission David was not able to go to meet Prema madam everyday for a longer time. So,

David said to his parents that he wanted to take tuition from her new teacher. His parents didn't think more and allowed him to do the same.

David started taking tuition from Prema. They like each other. They fall in love. Now the tuition time became longer and by mutual understanding they became ready for the intercourse and they did it. The change in the behaviour and activities of Prema and David was noticed by the students and this message was spreading among students of class 11. This message was now reaching into the ears of other teachers also. Many times Prema protected David in highly indisciplined activities. It continued for 2 years till that student passed the school. David passed class 12th board examination.

Prema started making distance from him and shifted her house from that locality to a newly rented apartment flat.

She clearly told him that she does not want to maintain their affair because she is going to be married soon.

Prema's marriage ceremony was fixed now. She invited all the teachers. I also attended her marriage ceremony. She was now the second hand wife of that person who loved him a lot.

****

9. Betrayed

Mr. D'souza was my friend. He was not a fast friend but he was a good friend. He resided with me as a room partner for 3 years. Both of us were studying for job purposes. Mr. D'souza was very fond of eating non vegetarian but I have kept a condition in front of him that if you want to be my partner then you will never eat non vegetarian food in the room. He agreed after a long thinking. Both of us were studying well and living happily. He discussed all his family life and problems with me. He asked me also for help and I have given good suggestions to him many times. I was studying in an institute where many girls were there.

One day I was talking to my girlfriend on cell phone and I discussed something with him about my girlfriend then he told me that - you are making me jealous because I am not having any girlfriend. I said - this is not true. I was discussing it only because you are my good friend. He was very lazy in all the work. He always liked to sleep.

I got a good job in a good organization then he told me you never think for me. You worshiped your God willingly everyday and got a good job. But you did not request your God for me to give me a job. I was having a small picture of my God then he told me to sell it to him. I completely denied, then he told me, " Please request your God for me also. I really requested my god for him also and he also got a job. He became very happy and started dancing in the room.

Now he was going to be married. One day I told him that your sister in law will be my girlfriend then he became annoyed with me. He had lots of planning. He was very happy because as soon as he got a government job his marriage was fixed. He Invited me to his marriage ceremony. I saw his wife was very beautiful. The marriage ceremony took place there and we returned back to our home. After a few days I heard that his wife ran away with someone on the first night itself after the marriage ceremony and returned back to home after one month. It was very bad luck for Mr. D'souza . He was supposed to divorce her but he didn't. He forgave her due to defaming. It was a very big mistake.

His wife was having an affair with someone else for many years. She didn't like Mr. D'souza because of his dark complexion. She got married to him only due to family pressure. Girl's family knew everything about her in spite of knowing the fact they forcibly married her with Mr. D'souza .

Mr. D'souza was in a very big tension but he did not discuss these things with his friends because he was feeling ashamed. His wife was a second hand wife for him. She didn't allow him for any intercourse in spite of being a second hand wife.

She became pregnant. The issue in her womb was of her boyfriend. Mr. D'souza knew everything but he didn't tell anyone. She gave birth to a baby after a few months.

Mr. D'souza was very happy and told everyone that he has become father of a very beautiful daughter. For 3 years Mr. D'souza lived happily with his daughter. In between his wife was leaving her house for two three days many times without any notice and returned back. He was taking care of his daughter very well. Many times He made a call to me and discussed his daughter. He was very happy. I saw his daughter. She was really beautiful. His daughter was now 4 years old.

A very bad day came into the life of Mr. D'souza . During Corona time he got sick. His wife didn't take care of him and left him to God. She did not give a single medicine to him. He died at home.

He was in a government job so after a few days the government offered his wife a job in government. She joined the job and owned the whole property of Mr. D'souza . Now she has started living happily with her boyfriend.

She didn't repent much of his death because she was a second hand wife.

Mr. D'souza was supposed to divorce her on the first night when she ran away with her previous lover but he didn't.

He died only because he accepted a second hand wife.

****

10. Hope Mine

Chunky was a poor person. I have seen him since his childhood. I was also a child at that time. He was not very good in study but he was a laborious person in his life.

His first job was in a hotel. He was going everyday and in the morning and coming back home late at night.

Sometimes he was doing night duty. It was a very small hotel, not a bigger one. Now he has become a mature person so his family wants to arrange his marriage with someone.

Chunky got married to a very dark complexion lady named Paro. He also had a dark complexion but his looks were better than his wife Paro. After one year she gave birth to a baby. The baby was also of very dark complexion. Both the members Chanky Babu and his wife were not happy with the colour of their daughter but they accepted and loved the baby because she was their first child.

That lady wife of Chunky was in love with someone before being married and that person was very smart. He came to live in the same colony in her neighbourhood. She became very happy after seeing her love Arun in the neighbourhood.

Her love started again and reached an extreme point. Whenever Chunky was going for night duty in his hotel, Paro started sleeping with previous lover Arun.

After one year Paro again gave birth to a very smart white complexioned son.

Chunky and Paro both were very happy after seeing their son because the sun was of very bright complexion. Chunky was very surprised to see the son. A little bit of confusion was there in his mind because the daughter was very dark complexioned and the son was opposite to it with white complexion.

Now his son was growing day by day.

His face was now very clear and it was not matching with Chunky and Paro. It was clearly visible that the face of the son was matching with their neighbour Arun.

One day Chunky Babu asked Paro how it is possible that the face of their son is matching with his neighbour. Paro replied it is possible, and sometimes it happens if while waking up in the morning you see a very good face every day that comes in your child.

So I was doing it and it happened.

You can also read in different magazines it is given. Because of this reason you can see at many houses that a pregnant lady pastes posters of very smart child's on the wall in their bedroom. Chunky has seen it in many houses so he believed that his son is white complexioned due to this reason. When his son became two years old his face was clearly matching with the neighbour Arun. Some of the friends of Chunky started discussing among themselves about the face of the child not matching with Chunky and somehow it came into the ears of Chunky and Paro. Chunky became very unhappy. He decided to leave that colony and left that colony.

His wife gave birth to two children, both of them were fine. Both of them were bright and both of them did shine. Chunky hoped - they are mine.

He shifted into another colony.

He left his hotel job and started selling and purchasing land for others. In this job maximum time he was residing at his home only. He was doing this business from his home.

All it happened due to Paro, his second-hand wife.

But everything is alright now in the new colony. His sons are now studying in a college.

****

11. Power

This is the story of a newly established colony. Robert was a new renter in the colony. He was in a private job. He bought a small plot in that colony and made his house. He made friendship with David, the criminal brother of the landlord who sold his plot to him. David knew everyone in that area because he was a local person. David helped him in making his house by arranging different items for the house at a cheaper rate.

Robert was very happy because he saved lots of money due to David's help during building his house. When Robert was on duty David was helping his wife also for the requirement of necessary items of the house. David was wasting his lots of time gossiping with Robert's wife. Robert and his wife both trusted David a lot.

Now Robert was thinking that he is also very powerful because of his friendship with that criminal. Robert was going to his job in a company everyday in the morning and coming back home in the evening. Sometimes he was getting night duty also. He was living happily with his wife and a very cute toddler daughter.

After a few months of building his house, one day his sister in law Julie came to live with them. She came to see their newly built house and started staying with them. She was a very beautiful teenager. Her face was so attractive that anyone could be watchful for hours. I saw her and I was also attracted. I liked her but I was not having enough time to go to her house and meet her. David saw her in the house of David and fell in love at first sight.

David started coming to Robert's house so often. He started gossiping with his sister in law also. Now David was bringing some edible items of her choice everyday to lure her. Robert's whole family was very happy with David because they were thinking that he is taking lots of care of his family.

But it was just like nourishing a tree before plucking its fruits or a cat was guarding the milk. Robert's sister in law Julie was also now attracted towards David. Both of them were in love with each other and they were gossiping a lot everyday in the same house. Robert and his wife were unaware of it; they were taking it very lightly.

One day when Robert was on duty in his company David came to meet his family. Robert's wife was taking a bath in the bathroom so Julie opened the door of the house. David entered the house. He saw that Robert was not there, his wife was in the bathroom and the toddler daughter was sleeping. This was the golden time for David to express his love to Julie. He hugged Julie and she was also very happy. Both of them started loving and kissing each other. David overpowered her and made intercourse with her. She opposed but did not shout due to fear of defaming the colony, and she did not support him willingly. Being in love with David was her blundering mistake. For the whole she was repenting a lot. But everything has gone. She was in the pool of tears. David moved away. Robert's wife came out from the bathroom then his sister started crying and narrated this to her. She was totally surprised because she trusted David a lot. She was depending on David for small things also. How can David do this?.

Robert came in the evening from duty. Everything was normal at his home because his wife did not discuss this to him at that time. They had dinner happily. His sister in law was not happy at the time of dinner so Robert asked her why she was not happy. His wife changed the matter. When they went to sleep ,at that time Robert's wife discussed this bad incident to her husband. Her husband was full of anger and told - I am going to kill him right now. Robert's wife said this is not the right time. We will do it in the morning. Robert was full of tension. He didn't sleep the whole night. He was waiting to take revenge. In the morning Robert became ready to go to fight with him. Then his wife said, wait for a few minutes, we cannot hit him in his area so we should call him at our house.

They made a call to David and called him for a meeting for an important discussion.

Since David has done everything wrong with Julie, so he knew why they were calling. He came totally prepared for any kind of fight. David reached their house, rang the bell. Robert opened the door and started shouting at him. Robert tried to hit him then David took out his gun and told that he is a criminal and powerful person of that area so no one can harm him.

After seeing his gun Robert's family totally became scared. Robert's wife interfered and cooled down both Robert and David and told David not to come to the house anymore.

David went back at that time.

After a few days David again came to their house when Robert was on duty. Robert's wife saw him so she did not open the door and told to go back. But David was a very cunning person. He said that he came here only to say sorry and ask forgiveness. David started weeping, and said sorry. It was totally crocodile tears. Robert's wife saw this and she opened the door. David entered the house and after a few minutes he took out his gun again and forcibly molested Julie. David told them that if they discuss these things with anyone he will kill the whole family. He also said he will come every afternoon with his gun for the same thing and if they are not ready for his misdeed then he will defame them in the colony. He continued the next day also.

Robert's wife did not tell this to her husband because there would be a big fight and anything very harmful would be there.

So she called her brother and without discussing those bad events she sent her sister Julie back to the village.

Next day in the afternoon David again came to Robert's house but he did not find Julie. He asked - where Julie?

Today Robert's wife was very happy. She said she went back to her village and she is going to be married very soon. David went back forever with sadness.

****

12. Misfortune

This is the story of a village. There was a girl named Sara. She was a young girl living with her family.

She had a very big family of 12 members: five brothers, five sisters, her mother and father. She was the elder sister out of 10 brothers and sisters. She was not highly educated. She studied up to middle school only. As she became 18 years old then her whole distant family members, neighbours and relatives gave pressure on her father to get her married somewhere because many younger sisters and brothers were also there after her.

Her father tries to find a groom for her and somehow he finds a groom for her named Shiva. His village was very far from their own village. Shiva was not doing any job because he was studying for graduation. He was tall and smart. The date of the marriage ceremony got fixed. All the family members were busy in the arrangement of different things for the marriage ceremony. The date of marriage came. All those persons whom her family knew were invited to the marriage ceremony. I was invited so I went to attend the marriage ceremony. Everything was going smoothly. The event was completed and Sara reached her in-laws house.

First year of marriage life came to an end in a normal way just like a poor family. Sara didn't like it. She started putting pressure on her husband for a good job so that they can enjoy life well, which was necessary also.

Shiva was not getting any job and his family was not buying necessary household items for their livelihood

because of poverty. Sara was sad because sometimes she was not having bath soap, toothpaste, detergent etc.
Sara and Shiva both were not happy in married life because they were depending on their parents for every small thing which they didn't like.
Shiva was tired of these everyday problems so he decided to leave his house and go to another state for some kind of job. Shiva left his house and reached Allahabad by train and without ticket. There he tried to find a job but he didn't get any. He was sitting under a tree near Ganga river in Allahabad. He was hungry. A saint saw him and understood his condition by mere observation only. He reached Shiva and offered some fruits to him. Shiva was very hungry so he consumed the fruit. The saint asked him why he was sitting here in this condition. Shiva narrated his whole story to him. The saint told him that he will not get any good job in the city because of the unemployed crowd. He suggested Shiva to become a saint, he also told that you will get enough food and money everyday into this life. Shiva got ready for this. The saint took him to the saint society. There Shiva became a complete saint. They hypnotized and counselled Shiva to not to return to his house.
Sara was in deep distress because Shiva disappeared from his own house. The whole family members of Sara and Shiva were in search of Shiva but they didn't get him.
One year completed, Shiva did not return to his home. Elder brother of Shiva started giving all the household necessary items to Sara. Shiva's brother tries to make Sara happy. He offered her some kind of love and affection

which Sara accepted because she was a newly married lady and she was deprived of some kind of love. Both of them fall in love with each other and Sara starts enjoying her married life and intercourse with his elder brother. Both of them were very happy and Sara became a second hand wife for him and forgot her original husband Shiva. Her relationship was illegal but It continued for many years.

After 10 years Shiva returned back to his home and tried to talk to Sara. Shiva's elder brother refused to identify him as his brother.

He also counselled Sara not to identify him as her husband because if he comes back home then he will know each and everything and then it will be a huge problem for Sara.

So Sara refused to identify him. Sara told he is a stranger and she doesn't know him.

Shiva returned back to saint life forever.

Now Sara is living happily with her illegal second husband in the village.

****

13. Greedy People

Eliza, a young girl, married at the age of 18 years. Her father has given dowry for this arranged marriage. Everyone was happy with the marriage in Eliza's family.

But as soon as Eliza reached in - laws house the problem started from there. Her mother in law did not like her and her father in law was a slave of her mother in law. so he also did not like her. He was doing all his activity following the statement of his wife. And when mother and father in laws both are not accepting the newly married bride then how the other family members will like her. They were very greedy and the worst people. It came to know that they were doing the marriage of their son only for the dowry. They have done this earlier also with a girl, Eliza was the second prey for them. Their main aim was to get lots of gold and money. Her husband was also helping his parents in this misdeed. The whole family was greedy.

Eliza's husband did not like her and started torturing from the first day. For every small thing she was being scolded at in law's house. Sometimes she was being scolded for those mistakes also which she had not done. They tortured her up to that extent that she was willing to leave her in -laws house all the time.

After one year she gave birth to a very beautiful baby. Her husband and mother in law both started torturing her a lot because she has given birth to a baby and they were willing to have a male child. They forced her to go back to her mother. They also told her if she will not go by herself they will kick her outside the home. She was crying but no one listened to her hue and cry. He made a call to her family member and disclosed all these things.

Next day When her father came to meet her she described all these things to her father and said that she wanted to go back to her own home. Her father agreed and brought his daughter home.

Eliza narrated all the stories of her torture at her in-laws house to her mother. Her mother became very sad and after listening to all these things decided that Eliza will not go back to her in-laws house. Her in-laws also said that there is no need to return Eliza back.

One year was going to be completed but from the in-law's house they never asked about Eliza, they forgot Eliza forever. Other neighbours suggested the remarriage of Eliza with a good person because mother and father will not be alive to help her at old age. Eliza's father agreed over it and started looking for a good person who will be ready willingly for the marriage with Eliza after knowing each and everything about her.

Here on the other side a person named James was living with his two toddler children. Wife of James was not alive; she died a few months back due to some critical diseases. James was looking for any lady who could be ready to marry him but the condition he kept was that she had to nourish his two children.

Father of Eliza was very worried about the future and life. He was also searching for a new groom for her who can marry Eliza after knowing all the stories. Somehow he came to know about James and the next day he went to meet James. First of all he listened to everything from

James himself. After knowing the complete story of James he also described the pain of his daughter and narrated all the story that happened to her.

He put a proposal in front of James to be married with his daughter Eliza. James asked him to give some time for thinking. He said OK. After a few days James sent a message to father of Eliza for the acceptance of his proposal of remarriage of James and Eliza.

Both the families of Eliza and James became very happy and got ready for the marriage of Eliza and James. They got married and both of them are living very happily. The children of each other were getting love from mother and father both and are growing very well. Eliza was a second wife and James was a second husband for each other but all were very happy. Their family members are also very happy. This is very happy ending to their story.

****

14. Trapped

This is the story of a nice colony and well off families residing there. A Government officer was residing in the colony with whole family members including three daughters. They all were very beautiful. They were having such a kind of beauty that if they are passing through anywhere you cannot stop your eyes from looking at them. They were very famous in the locality for their beauty. Some of the youth were coming by motorcycle from three kilometres away to have a look at them.

I was residing there in the same colony. I was also a big fan of their beauty. I really liked one of them named Gabriella. She was more beautiful than the other two sisters. She was two years younger than me in study. See never came out alone from her house so that I can propose to her. She was always coming out along with her sisters. So I never got any opportunity to propose to Gabriella.. Many times I threw letters in her home but I didn't get any reply from her. I tried a lot but didn't get success and my feelings for her died in my heart.

My one of the neighbours named Jonathan, who was senior to me and residing near us on rent, started going to meet her father unnecessarily only to make friendship with him. Jonathan started doing some of the household work to impress his father and to be there in his good book. He started bringing newspapers, vegetables and other household items for them as a helper. He started working for them just like a servant.

Jonathan was wasting and investing his lot of time for this. All three beautiful sisters started talking to him and going with him for shopping and some other work. Gabriela and one of her sisters together started liking Jonathan.

Jonathan was investing his time for Gabriella only. One day he proposed to Gabriela and she accepted his proposal because she was also in love with him.

Gabriella started sometimes going alone with Jonathan for shopping, college and at many places. Jonathan was very happy because whatever he wanted to get he has achieved it. He has discussed all these things with his friends. Jonathan was a very cunning person. He was having a very bad plan in his mind for Gabriella which she never realized.

One day when Gabriella asked Jonathan to drop up to her college then you became ready and moved along with her to the college. On the way Jonathan made a request to Gabriela to bunk her college and enjoy an outing the whole day with him. Gabriella became ready for that after some hesitations and discussions. Firstly they moved to the zoo. They were in the zoo for two hours. After that they took some snacks and cold drinks and made a plan to go somewhere else. Jonathan told her to take a rest for half an hour at his friend's room which is nearby the zoo.

Gabriella clearly denied this but after making lots of requests from Jonathan she became ready for that. When Gabriella reached his friend's room he offered a cold drink and some table items. She denied consuming this but due to lots of requests and pressure she consumed it. After consuming a cold drink Gabriella became unconscious there. Jonathan has put some sleeping pills into the cold drink. All these things were totally planned by Jonathan. He molested her physically in her unconsciousness. He did very wrong with Gabriella.

After sometime when Gabriella woke up she realized that Jonathan had looted her modesty.

****

15. A Courageous Lady

This is the story of a newly made state. Government has given vacancies for many posts in abundance. A newly married couple Mr Michael and Mrs. Julia applied for the post of teacher. They appeared in an interview but Mr Michael only passed it. He joined as a primary teacher there. Government appointed him in a remote area far from the city. His school was 25 kilometres away from the main city. The mode of transport was also not available there. It was very difficult for Mr Michael to go there every day and come back in the evening because of the unavailability of a transport facility. He decided to stay in the village on rent. But in that village no one was ready to give their house on rent. Their house was also in a poor condition. All the families were not having toilets in their house. They were going to the cropping fields for defecation in the morning. It was very difficult for Mr Michael so he was looking for a house on rent with a toilet facility in the village which was not available. He started living on the school campus itself. After dispersal school was vacant and there was a toilet also. He asked villagers for a plot if anyone wanted to sell. Because he wanted to buy and to make a house for him there. After sometime one of the villagers was in need of money so he sold his plot to Mr Michael. He bought the plot and started making his house there. Some of the Villagers were very helpful. The construction of the house was completed in a year with the help of villagers. Earlier Mr Michael was living alone in the village so it was very difficult for him to cook food for both the times. Now Mr Michael brought his wife Julia also there. They were living happily in that village also where no facility of hospital, post office etc was available. No market was there. Only one grocery shop was there which was also very small. But like other villagers he also managed to live there. They were having two children and both were boys.

One day when they were sleeping at midnight some of the robbers attacked his house. Mr Michael fought with him but robbers murdered him and robbed his house. Mrs Julia ran out of the house and started shouting for help. She was scared and screaming. villagers came out for help within a few minutes but all the robbers ran away. Mrs Julia became a widow. She was very scared. She decided to leave the village immediately. All the villagers made a request to her to stay there, they promised to help her all the time. But she was not ready to stay in the village. She locked her house and left the village with her children. Villagers helped her in reaching the bus stand and nearby City. Villagers also told her that whenever you want to come back we are always there for your help please don't forget us. Mrs Julia reached her parents and told them everything. Her whole family was in deep distress. I personally visited that village once due to some urgent work but after that I never wanted to go there.

They all filed an FIR against the robbers and informed all the government officials about the murder of Mr Michael. District education officer thought about how Mrs Julia would survive with her children without any job. They decided to offer the same job to Mrs Julia because it was in the government rule also that if anyone dies his job will be transferred to his wife or the nominee. After a few months the district education officer sent a joining letter to Mrs Julia in the same school on the same post.

She was not ready to go to that village for the job. But her parents asked her how she will take care of both the children without money.

Many kinds of expenditures are there which she had already seen. She told her parents to give her some time to think about it. She agreed after some time and decided to leave both the children in a boarding school hostel in the City. Her parents ask how you will live alone in that village. She replied I have lost my husband so I cannot take a chance for my children. I have decided to live alone in that house in the village and villagers are very helpful. They have promised me for help. Parents said okay as you wish but take care of yourself and make a call to us whenever you are in need. Mrs Julia said okay and went there to join the same school as a primary teacher.

When she joined that school, villagers became very happy. They told all of us to be ready for your help all the time. Every night one person will sleep outside your house for safety. She said, nothing is there in my house. Robbers have robbed everything. After that every day she started going to school which was just 100 meters away from her house. Every night one powerful person of the village started sleeping in her house for her safety. She agreed about it. She fell in love with him and started enjoying her life with him. Every person of that village came to know about her relationship with some powerful persons of the village but they did not speak anything. Mrs Julia continued her job there with the help of those Villagers.

In between during different vacations children were coming to live with their mother. But she did not allow them to stay for a longer period in the village. During summer vacation Mrs. Julia was also going to meet her parents in the City. She was enjoying her summer vacation with the children in her parental house in the City. Both her sons are adults now. Time to time they go to meet their dear mother.

Now she is going to retire from the job .

****

16. Hanged his wife

This is the story of Mr Alexander. He was in the Police force. He was working well and earning well. He got married to Miss Claire. They were living in a rented flat in Chennai.

He was living happily with his wife. After a few years his wife became pregnant. For a few months she did all her household work but after that it became very difficult for her to do all kinds of work. So she made a request to her husband to bring a lady for her help. He said ok I'll arrange someone. He tried to find out but didn't get anyone. At last he told his wife to call her sister. Claire said OK I will make a request to her to come here for my help. Next day Claire made a call to her sister Olivia. She made lots of requests for her to come for help. Olivia became ready to help her sister and next day Mr Alexander went to her house to bring her along with him. Olivia came with him. She was helping her sister Claire well. Mr Alexander and Olivia came very close during these days because all the household work was being done by Olivia. For each and everything Mr Alexander was depending on Olivia now. Both of them fell in love with each other. When Claire was sleeping Mr Alexander and Olivia started enjoying each other's love which was totally wrong.

The day came when Claire gave birth to a beautiful baby. All were very happy because a new guest had come to the house as a baby. Soon the baby became three months old. Claire asked Olivia to go back to your home because parents were waiting. Olivia discussed it with Mr Alexander then he started shouting at Claire and said baby is very small how you will be able to do all the household work alone. So please let Olivia stay here for some more time. Claire said OK. Mr Alexander became very happy because Olivia was going to stay for some more time. He was in love with Olivia and wanted to marry her. Olivia was also ready for the same. One day Mr Alexander proposed to Olivia for marriage. Olivia said I am also ready but it is not possible because you are already a married person with my sister. Mr Alexander said I promise that I will marry you one day. Olivia laughed at him and said don't be a fool and please stop daydreaming. After one year Claire saw Olivia and Alexander together in love. She was astonished but didn't say anything at that time. She understood the sensitivity of their relationship. Later on when Alexander went for duty Claire started shouting at Olivia and said that you are destroying my happy life. You're destroying your elder sister's life. Please move away from my life unless I will disclose your matter to our parents and all the relatives. Olivia was scared of the defaming because he was an unmarried girl. She said ok tomorrow I will leave. Mr Alexander came back from duty , then Olivia said I want to go back to my village because my parents are waiting there. Claire said yes she is right, our baby has also become one year old and she is able to walk by herself thanks to Olivia. Alexander please leave her up to her village she is also willing to go.. Alexander was surprised and in shock. He was thinking how Olivia could be ready to go. He became upset and left Olivia to her village. But he made a promise to Olivia that very soon she will be his wife.

Mr Alexander came back to Claire at his home. Everything became normal and Alexander and Claire started living happily like earlier. But Alexander was having very bad planning in his mind.

He was living in a single floored rented house. Everyday Alexander was going to bring milk in the morning. Just after three months of the dispersal of Olivia, Alexander hanged his wife early in the morning in her bedroom. Her baby was sleeping. He locked his room from inside, and moved to the roof. He jumped down from the roof at the back of his house and went to bring milk. He came after half an hour with milk and started shouting in front of his house for help from neighbours. He said that his wife has locked the flat from inside and she is not opening it. He was out bringing milk. Neighbours suggested breaking the door. He broke the door with the help of neighbours and entered the house with neighbours. All of them saw that his wife was hanging from the ceiling. Mr Alexander started crying and saying that his wife was not happy with a girl child so she hanged herself. It was totally false and he was showing crocodile tears. They called police and filed an FIR. Police personnel made a query with neighbours then everything was in support of Mr Alexander because he had broken the door with the help of neighbours and everyone had seen his wife was hanging. They took the statement of Mr Alexander. He also gave his statement against Claire. The investigation took place. The file was closed because police had written that it is matter of suicide.

Just after one month of this incident he convinced his father in law that it is not possible for him to nourish his daughter alone and no one else except Olivia. She can take care of his baby. His father in law allowed it because Olivia was having an affair with one of the youth in her village. He wanted Olivia to go somewhere and Olivia was also ready to live with Alexander.

Mr Alexander got married with Olivia and started living together.

****

17. The Nurse

This is the story of a nurse named Emily. An old lady became very sick. She was in need of a nurse for her help all the time 24x7. Her son Mr James went to a nearby hospital. He discussed the matter with the hospital manager and asked for a nursing assistant at home. He said ok and sent Emily at his home for the service of that old lady, who was the mother of Mr James. Emily started doing her service. Mr James and his mother both were happy with her service. The whole family of Mr James was happy with her service. Emily was always smiling which everyone liked. His mother got well and returned back to the village.

Wife of Mr James was not living with him all the time she was residing at her village. Mr James was rarely going to the village to meet his family. He falls in love with Emily. Mother of Mr James became well and reached to her village. Mr James and Emily both were in love. Emily continued coming to meet him every day. Mr James gave her proposal of marriage. Emily accepted his proposal and got married in a temple. They did not call any of the guests because Mr James was already married and father of four children. He has disclosed everything to Emily. In spite of that she was ready for marriage because Emily had affairs with many people but they all betrayed her. Mr James knew that Emily had affair with many people. But his love was blind so he married her. Very soon Emily gave birth to a male child. They were living happily. One day I reached to meet him, Emily became very happy that at least one guest came to meet them after their marriage. She served me also very well. The whole family of Mr James was now unhappy with her and started hating her. The family of Mr James in the village started some planning to separate them but did not successes.

Mr. James bought a new house and put lots of effort in decorating it. Finally the house was ready to move. He organised a big party on this occasion and invited all his relatives. The function was about to start then his elder son came there.

He was very angry with him because he knew that his father had married another lady and he had a child with her and he didn't invite his son in the function.

He reached his flat at the function and beat him badly. Mr James was in deep distress because his son has hit him today. Emily consoled him and called some rowdy people to take revenge from son of Mr James but he ran away. The family of Mr James did not lodge an FIR because they didn't want to send Mr James to jail.

One day Emily visited my city and she made me a call to meet me. I went there to meet her. She told me that she has come with the purpose of tourism. She asked about the list of tourist places from me. I gave her the idea of tourist places and came back. At that time Google was not working. I went to meet her again in the late evening at her flat then I saw that she was Indulge with someone else in a love affair. It was totally unaccepted. Emily looked at me and made lots of requests to me not to disclose her matter with Mr James. I told her that I will not disclose but you are not a good lady.

****

18. The Marriage

There was a girl named Amelia in a village. Her family was very poor. Amelia was a growing child. She grew up and became 18 years old. She was at that age of marriage. Her family was not able to do any kind of expenditure at her marriage ceremony. They kidnapped a boy named William of the same religion, brought him home and married him firstly with Amelia in front of all the villagers. William was not a brilliant person, he did not study well. He was of average intelligence. Amelia's father reached to William's father and started crying that he has made a blundering mistake. He had kidnapped his son William and married him with his daughter Amelia. Some villagers were also with them. They all started begging pardon for him. He was a very kind person but became very angry because they have kidnapped his child and married without permission. Since all the villagers were begging for pardon, he forgave them. He went to the village of Amelia's father with some of the relatives and brought Amelia as his daughter in law with respect. He threw a party in the village because his elder son has got married and daughter in law has come.

After a few months Amelia understood that her husband is of average intelligence. She was not satisfied with him in her married life.

She started looking for someone else for enjoyment of her life. She was deprived of a strong intelligent mail person's love. Firstly, she offered her love to her uncle. Har uncle accepted her proposal and they started enjoying it together at night. One day Mr William saw that Amelia is enjoying with someone else. He understood that he has got a second hand wife and he complained about this to his elder's at home and hit her.

For a few days Amelia became quiet and after that she offered her love to cousins of William. They also accepted her proposal and started enjoying it with Amelia. One day her mother in law saw this and slapped very tightly. She said sorry and became quiet for a few days. After that again she started enjoying it with a new cousin in the in-laws house itself. Amelia became a characterless daughter-in-law. After a few years she gave birth to three children one by one. After that she became very busy with children and forgot to do all these things.

****

19. The Love Birds

This is the story of love birds of a reputed school of a mega city. Two students Chris and Chloe who were in love from class 10th.Now They were studying in class 11th and both of them were minors. Chloe was a very beautiful girl but not having a sharpened mind. Chris was also average in study and he was also not a smart child. In starting only Chris was having one sided love for Chloe.

Many times Chris decided to propose to her but he knew that she did not like him so he did not propose. Chloe's father was having his posting in another City, so Chloe was residing with her mother only. She was single child of her parents.

One day Chris asked Chloe to study together for class 12th board examinations. Chloe agreed to study together but she clearly told him that I will not come to your home because my mother is very strict and you will also not come to my home. Now think well what to do?

Chloe suggested that you can come to my home in the evening when my mother is not present there because in the morning we are always there in school. Every day in the evening my mother is going to bring milk from the nearby cowshed and she comes back after one hour because she enjoys gossiping with her friends and evening walk. Chris asked her to start from today itself. Chloe said okay and he started coming for study. They were studying well and sometimes they were talking about love affairs etc. due to their adolescence period. Both of them now fell in love but they were not proposing to each other. One day after studying for half an hour they were talking about love affairs and they also started touching and kissing each other.

Now it has become their everyday affair. They also promised each other that they will not disclose it to anyone. Day by day their love was growing bigger and they were curious to do something more but Chloe was denied for it. One day what happened to Chloe was that she agreed to do something more and they enjoyed the intercourse after that Chloe felt very ashamed and started crying. Chris asked her to forgive him and kneeled down on her feet to say sorry. He was begging for forgiveness. Now it was time to leave so he left her house. Next day, Chloe was not talking to him in the school. He promised her that he will never disclose this thing to anyone so not to worry. She forgave him and he was again willing to go to her house to study. Next day in the evening he reached her house and knocked on the door Chloe was scared but she opened the door.

Chris entered her house and started studying. Chloe try to forget the previous matter and started studying with him. She continued studies with him. One day Chris asked for a glass of water, she went to bring water from the kitchen then he fixed his mobile camera in her room. When she brought water for him after consuming water he hugged Chloe, said thank you for water and started kissing her.

Chloe asked what happened why you are doing like this?

He replied let us enjoy it only once more, like earlier please, please. Chloe said no you have promised you will not to do this.

Chris said only for today I am begging you after this I will never do anything and did the wrong thing with her after overpowering. Chloe started crying and said you have betrayed. I will never talk to you. He said sorry and left the house with his mobile phone.

Now Chris was not given attention to study even in school and became busy watching that video all the time. He stopped going to her house to study because he was busy watching that video.

After a few days he again reached Chloe's house but she said she would not open the door today and ask him to go back. He said okay I will go back but I want to show you something before that. Chloe said okay show me that video from the window and after seeing that immediately see opened the door and started crying and asked him to delete it.

He said he will delete it today in front of her after enjoying love with her. Chloe became ready for that unwillingly. Chris enjoyed it and told her that he will enjoy it with her everyday so he will not delete and leave the house. Chloe was repenting on her mistake to allow him to study. He started coming and enjoying every day with her.

One day some of the neighbours complained to Chloe's mother that every day in the evening someone is coming to her home for one hour in the evening when she is not present at her home, which they don't feel good about. She said okay I will see the matter. She went to her home and asked her daughter about it. Chloe started crying and told everything to her mother about that video clip also and told he is blackmailing her and coming everyday to molest her.

Her mother also dipped in tears and said let him come today and after that he will never be able to come. Her mother hid herself in the room with a thick stick in the evening. As soon as Chris reached her home and started molesting Chloe. Her mother came out and beat him badly with the stick. She broke the mobile into pieces and started shouting thief, thief, thief. All the neighbours gathered and they also beat Chris. After that they called the police and handed him over to the police on the charge of theft in the house. Chris was not able to speak anything and moved with the police. He accepted the charge of theft because he knew that the charge of molestation would give him a much tougher punishment than theft. Since he was a student, after a few days police forgave him and released him after signing a bond paper that he will never do it again in future. The police also warned his parents and told to take care.

He did not disclose that matter to anyone. But all the school friends knew about the matter which he did not disclose due to fear of jail.

Chloe's mother did not return his mobile phone and threw it in the gutter. Chloe was very happy today. She hugged her mother and said thank you for saving her. She saved her daughter in a tricky way. Chloe's mother stopped her evening walk and wherever she was going she was taking Chloe also with her. During board examinations everyday Chloe's mother was sitting on the gate of the school. After the board examination they left the city forever and moved to that city where her father was posted. Whenever she will be married she will be a second hand wife unwillingly.

*****

20. A Fake Love

This is the story of a nice colony where more than a thousand people were residing. Generally it happens that some of the relatives come to reside with us during summer vacation. There was a person named Daniel living in that colony. In the neighbourhood of Daniel a girl named Luna came to live with her relatives. Luna was short heighted girl. One of her eyes was acquainted. Despite that, she was looking beautiful. I am fond of having different kinds of flowers in my garden. One day Luna came to me and asked me for some flowers and plants in the evening. I told her that we always uproot plants during the day, not in the evening. She said okay and went back. Next day she came to me in the morning and asked for the plants, then I gave her some plants. She became very happy and went back.

Luna was a teenage girl. She started liking Daniel who was residing beside her flat. Daniel was young and smart but an unmarried gentleman. Daniel was a graduate and looking for a job. He was busy thinking about his job only. Every day he was roaming on the top floor of his house in the evening. He notices that Luna is attracted to him. For a few days he ignored it. He thought that he might be wrong. She could see something somewhere else. But when she continued then Daniel also started liking her. Both of them started talking with each other. Daniel was not satisfied by talking only. He was thinking of something more but it was not possible during the day or in the evening. Daniel made a request to her to meet at night when the whole colony will be sleeping. First day Luna refused but she agreed after two or three days. Luna said okay but I will not come to your house you will jump and come on my roof when I'll ask you to come. Daniel agreed. They fixed a meeting the next day at midnight. Daniel started waiting on his rooftop at the given time. Luna came a little late and asked him to jump over the roof. Daniel jumped and reached Luna. They enjoyed themselves a lot that night and came back early in the morning. When Daniel was coming back to his own roof then one of the neighbours saw him jumping from Luna's roof to his own roof. In the morning he came to meet Daniel's parents and complained about it. Daniel's parents asked him about the matter then he completely denied. His parents told him they never want to listen to this kind of complaint. Daniel said it is totally false. After the completion of summer vacation Luna went back to our Village. Next year she came to live in the neighbourhood again. But this time her husband was also there with her. But he never knew that.......

After a few years she stopped coming.

****

21. A Plot

This is the story of a village where a powerful person named Joseph was residing. He was a very rich person in the village. Joseph had two sons and a cousin brother. They all adult now. All were residing in the same home. It was a joint family. There were lots of work in the house of Mr Joseph. For every work he has recruited someone from the village who were coming to his home for doing different kinds of work and back to their home in the evening. But for washing clothes he had a washer man who did not have any place to live. Mr Joseph has given a small plot just beside his home to the washer man. He made a small Hut there and started living. In the family of the washer man, one daughter and son were there. His daughter named Supriya was not so beautiful but she was young. Many a times she was coming to collect clothes and to return their clothes. Supriya was a teenage girl. She was attracted to the son and cousin of Mr Joseph. She liked every adult in the family of Mr Joseph. Elder son of Mr Joseph named Samuel was also attracted towards Supriya. Earlier the cousin of Mr Joseph was in love with Supriya. He has enjoyed his love with Supriya many times. When he became tired of Supriya he left her. Now Samuel and Supriya were in love.

One day when Mr Joseph went outside with his wife and one of the sons and no one was there in his home except Samuel. Supriya came there to ask for clothes for washing. Samuel held her and kissed her. Supriya was also enjoying this. She did not deny. After a few minutes they enjoy intercourse. Supriya went back happily because she had a boyfriend from a rich family. Samuel had now enjoyed the taste of real love. He became fan of supriya's love. Whenever he saw Sophia in loneliness he enjoyed being with her.

One day, the cousin of Mr Joseph came to meet him and told that he wanted to make his own house beside his home. Mr Joseph sad okay you can proceed. He gave a new small plot to the washer man far from his house and make his own flat there. The matter of Supriya and Samuel was over now .Next year Supriya married someone in her own community..

****

22. The Love On The Roof

This is the story of a lower middle class family living in a colony nearby my housing society. There was a family headed by Mr Graham. There were four members in his family: mother, father, daughter and son. Mr Graham was living happily with his family. Mr Graham was a teacher; his son also became a teacher in a private school. Mr Graham's wife was a housewife and his daughter Sophia was studying in the college. Sofia was having an affair with a neighbour named Thomas. Everyday Sophia was walking on her roof. Thomas was also roaming on his rooftop. Both of them were talking from a distance. Sophia was giving different types of body gestures to attract him. Thomas was attracted towards her and he was in love with her.

I personally met Mr Graham and his son. He was my teacher also for six months. I have taken tuition from them. Mr Graham was a very honest person. Mr Graham and his son both were in a private school so they were not getting any kind of leave for different kind of their household work. A very few counted leaves were allowed to them.

One day one of the relative came to invite them in a marriage ceremony in the village. Mr Graham and his son denied to go because their organisation was not giving them enough leave for that. Mrs Graham and her daughter became ready to go to attend the marriage ceremony. But there was a question that who will cook food for Mr Graham and his son. Then Mrs. Graham told

She will go alone with her relative and the daughter Sophia will stay here with them so that the matter of cooking food will be solved. Mrs Graham went to the village to attend the marriage ceremony happily.

Next day Mr Graham and his son went for duty. After many days today Sophia was alone at home. So she made a call to Thomas and asked to come at her home if he is free. Thomas agreed to come and asked Sophia to open the back door. He didn't want to come from the front gate because people can see. He was afraid of other neighbours because they do not like love affairs.

Thomas came and entered Sophia's house through the back door and started enjoying his love with Sophia. Unfortunately one of her neighbours saw that Thomas had entered Mr Graham house from the back door when Sophia was alone at home. He told all the neighbours that Sophia is alone at home and someone has entered her house. Within half an hour the neighbours gathered and decided to enter Sophia's house. They knocked on her door, Sophia was scared but there was no option so she opened the door. She saw all the neighbours on her door. She asked them what happened, uncle. Neighbours told we have seen someone has entered your house from the back door and since you are alone here, please let us check who has entered. Sophia said uncle Thomas has entered with my permission. He came here to meet me for some study purpose. Neighbours said we will not allow it, because Mr Graham is not here and you are alone so please send him outside. Thomas came out and moved to his home but he had enjoyed love with Sophia for more than half an hour. In the evening Mr Graham came back home and heard the whole story from his neighbours. He said thank you to all the neighbours. He entered into his house and started scolding Sophia for her misdeed. Her mother also came from the village and heard Sophia's story. She was feeling ashamed for Sophia.

Next year they fixed Sophia's marriage with someone.

****

23. Friendship

This is story of New Delhi. I was residing there..

Living in mega cities and maintaining friendship there is a very tough task. Lots of expenses are there. You cannot say your friends that you don't have money. First time I saw American friendship there. My all the friends decided to enjoy a party in a restaurant. I was not willing to go but under their lots of pressure we all moved to enjoy the party. We all enjoyed well. Everyone was giving order for himself. When the bill came, all the friends started collecting money and they paid the bill. This is known as American friendship, that enjoys together and pay separately. Jack and Sandra two friends were there. Both of them were in love with each other but they did not discuss it. All the time they were visible together. They were going college together and coming back together. One day another friend of Sandra named Elmer directly proposed and said I love you. She did not accept his proposal and told it to Jack. They said that Elmer is a fool. Many a times Jack made a request to Sandra to visit his rented flat but she denied. One day the college planned for a Tour. All the students became very happy. Jack and Sandra were also very happy.

When all the students were sleeping at night in the booked hotel God knows what they were talking till midnight. They were roaming together. They did shopping and took dinner in a restaurant. They enjoyed a lot in the excursion trip.

The college was closed now.

Sandra was free so she accepted Jacks request to visit his flat. She came around 12 o'clock in the afternoon to meet him. Jack was very happy today. He received Sandra on the bus stop and brought her to is flat. In his flat a room partner was already present there. When Sandra came and saw another person in the room she became upset and asked Jack how we will enjoy here you are already having room partner in your flat. Jack understood her opinion and said we will take lunch together and enjoy the gossiping only.

Sandra said ok and took lunch together and after that she wanted to go back. Jack said ok. He was going with Sandra up to bus stand. On the way Sandra asked for rupees Rs.2000. Jack said I don't have but what you will do with this money. Sandra said that she has to give it to someone. Jack left up to an auto and came back. It was an offer of enjoyment in lieu of Rs.2000. Jack felt that Sandra was not doing a good job. They continued their friendship but Jack never crossed his limit.

****

24. **A Blind Love**

This is the story of Alister and Elizabeth. There were one brother and two sisters. All were brilliant in their study but Elizabeth was extra brilliant. She was very cute. I came in touch with that family when Elizabeth was 7 years old only. Alister was 14 years old at that time and he was very smart in study and appearance both. I met her mother. She was also very beautiful, looking like Mrs World. Many times we met and gossiped. Alister was in love with a Punjabi girl named Gurdeep. Gurdeep was also very beautiful. Her face was round in shape. She was looking like a statue. Alister and Gurdeep continued their love for up to 4 years. As soon as Alister became class 12th student he gave a proposal to Gurdeep to run away with him and marry. Alister told her that after passing class 12th you will be taking admission somewhere else and I will be somewhere else so it will be not possible for us to meet and our love will be discontinued. Parents will also never agree for our marriage so we should run away and for marriage. Gurdeep agreed with him. Because they did not think about the future. They thought about their love only and one day there and away. They went to a temple and got married. For one day they enjoyed their first night at a friends flat which was vacant. Family of Gurdeep was not knowing about her affair with Alister so the informed all the relatives and lodged an FIR. They started searching Gurudev everywhere because they thought that she had been kidnapped. The informed about this incident to the school authority also so that they can help if they have any information.

On the second day after marriage they did not go anywhere else. Alister Brought her to his own house and told his mother that she is my wife and your daughter in law. His mother became very angry and slapped him; she also told Alister to leave her house immediately. But he was knowing her mother so he didn't go anywhere else and moved to his room. His mother started shouting who will marry your sisters if they know that you have kidnapped a girl and married her. You have become a criminal now. This is the crime to run away with a minor girl. Gurdeep's family would also be in trouble and tension. His mother took a blade and cut her own throat and she cut the throat of sisters Elizabeth and her elder sister both. Everywhere blood was there in her flat. Alisters mother was full of tension that her elder son was out of her hand. Everyone's throat was bleeding in the flat. His mother was not satisfied with this so she took kerosene oil and poured it on herself. She put herself on fire. Immediately all the neighbours came for help and sent the whole family to the hospital in emergency ward. Doctors helped well and they all came out of danger. I saw the cut mark on the throat of Elizabeth. Thank God they all were safe.

The matter was spreading over just like fire in the jungle. Then the parents of Gurdeep came to know that Gurdeep was there in the house of Alister. They moved there with the police and brought their daughter Gurdeep back. The police tried to arrest Alister but Gurdeep saved him. She gave his statement that she ran away with him by herself without any pressure. It was her choice because she loves him. Alister is not at fault. The police left him after signing a bond paper. Both of them are separated now. But first love never dies. Both of them appeared in the board examination but both of the brilliant students got poor results because of disturbance and their love.

Gurdeep's parents took her to Punjab and married her with someone. She became a second hand wife.

****

25. Two Friends

This is the story of that time When I was studying in a school. My two classmates Isabella and Jennifer were fast friends. Both of them were neighbours also in the same colony. Maximum time they were sitting and gossiping together. Jennifer was more beautiful than Isabella. She was as beautiful as a fairy but she was short heighted. Everyday both the friends were coming to school and going back together.

Isabella's elder brother named Charles started liking Jennifer and one day he proposed to her. She accepted his proposal. Both of them fall in love and start dating and meeting in the restaurant. Isabella was knowing all this things but she was not having courage to complain about it to her family. Jennifer also made a request to Isabella that she will not disclose her love to anyone.

One day Charles told Jennifer that they are not getting enough time for the love because all the neighbours keep vigil with them. They always watch past comments etc. Jennifer said it will happen in this society. People are like that only. They enjoy disturbing others' lives. Charles told her there is a proposal for you. Jennifer said don't give riddles and puzzles and asked to disclose it. Charles said we can move somewhere else for a few days after that when we will come back we will marry. Jennifer asked him are you okay?

Where will we stay if we run away? Charles said I have enough money. We will stay in a hotel , we will enjoy it together and come back. Both of them were looking at one side of the coin only. They did not think about what would happen in the family and society. Jennifer said okay, have a nice plan and tell me when we have to implement the plan. Charles said okay give me some time I will tell you everything. He met Jennifer in the evening and said tomorrow morning when you will go to school please pack your clothes in your bag in place of books and you will not enter the school campus. From the school gate we will move for next city. Jennifer said ok fine. Jennifer packed her bag with her clothes and other necessary items. She moved for school. Near the school gate Charles was waiting for her. They ran away from there. They took a train and moved to Goa.

After dispersal of school hours when Jennifer did not return home her family reached Isabella and started making lots of questions about Jennifer. In starting Isabella denied everything and she told Jennifer had not attended school today. She has not seen Jennifer in the school. Jennifer's parents were in shock that their teenage daughter was missing. Their whole family was crying.

They did not lodge an FIR because they told us we will be defaming this way and the police will not try to find our daughter.

Family of Isabella tried to find Charles in the late evening, then they saw that Charles was also missing at the same time. They started asking Isabella that you might have been hiding something. Please let the whole family know. Isabella was under the pressure of the whole family and they threatened to hit her. They started slapping Isabella then she spoke everything. She said that Charles and

Jennifer were both in love for the last few months. Charles has first proposed to her and they ran away together. But where they have gone that I don't know. They again slapped Isabella and told why you did not inform us earlier if you knew everything. Ishabela said that they have been told not to discuss it. They again slapped Isabella and said we are your parents, they are not.

Now the family of Isabella has confirmed that they have run together. They informed the family of Jennifer that Charles is also missing. He and Jennifer both were in love and they ran together. They also made a request to Jennifer's family not to lodge any FIR because only Charles will be in jail because Jennifer was a minor girl. They told ok we will not file FIR but please try to find out our daughter. Family of Isabella said yes we are trying to find out both of them.

On another side when Jennifer and Charles reached Goa they booked a double bedded room in a hotel in Goa. They checked in and started enjoying their life. They were taking sunbath on the Goa beach, and eating their favorite food in restaurants. It was the happiest day of their life. Whole day they were roaming in Goa, visiting different monuments, parts and different sea beaches and in the late evening coming back to the hotel. Within three days their money was replenished. Now they were worried what to do?

There was very little money with them. Charles said there is only one way that we have to return back to our home. Jennifer started crying. She asked Charles what about your money you have told me that you have enough money. Charles replied I did not know that within 3 days we will expand to 75000 rupees. Jennifer again started crying and said if you return back to our home how will I face our parents?

Now I am feeling very ashamed because I am able to understand what type of problems our parents would be facing in the colony. I have defamed my parents. I want to die here. I want to suicide here itself. Then Charles tried to make her understand and said that you are the only child of your family. If you will die then they will also die. They will not survive without you. You are the only hope of your parents. Children make mistakes but parents always forgive. Please return back home with me. If they will not accept you then I am ready to marry you in front of the whole colony then there will be no chance of defaming. Now Jennifer was ready to return home. Next day they took the train and returned back home.

Jennifer's parents became very happy after seeing their only daughter. Her mother hugged her and started crying and she also asked - why did you run away if you were in love with him? You were supposed to tell me. I am always ready for your marriage with him.

Now Jennifer was feeling more ashamed. Her father has stopped talking to her.

In the family of Charles when he returned back home they slapped Charles and told Jennifer was a minor girl you are not. If they would lodge an FIR your whole family would be in jail. Thanks to her parents that they did not file any FIR. Think about the pain of Jennifer's parents when she was missing without any information. They also told Charles that they will not give a single penny from their property if he will not forget Isabella. Charles was not having any job so he was not having any option with him. He obeyed his parents and forgot her.

When everything became normal Jennifer's parents changed their residence from that colony and shifted to another colony. Her mother told her that your only well-wishers are your parents. Tell us everything, we will manage. Jennifer passed her board examination and took an admission in another college. As soon as Jennifer became 18 years old her father married her in his own community and Jennifer did not deny it because Charles had stopped talking to her.

Jennifer became a second hand wife but no one came to know. She has two children now one boy and one girl. Her husband has left her because he was demanding some more dowry after the marriage also. I have not seen her husband from many years.

****

26. The Twins

This is the story of Dhanbad district. I came to know this story through my relatives because many close relatives are residing there. I also visited there many times and resided there for a few months. I came to know this story when a carpenter was doing some furniture making work at my house in Dhanbad.

The carpenter's name was Ravi and his brother's name was Abhi. They were twins, the face was hundred percent the same but behavioural attitude was different. Ravi has narrated his story to me by himself. Ravi and Abhi were from a poor family who did not have enough money. Abhi was working in Punjab in a small factory. In one year the first 6 months Abhi was working in that factory and Ravi was living in Dhanbad at home and for the next 6 months Ravi was working in the same factory and Abhi was living in Dhanbad at home. No one has observed even the factory owners were not aware of this. Both the brothers Ravi and Abhi were having a very good understanding of this.

Ravi has got a proposal to be married with a poor but beautiful girl named Joanna of his same community. Family of Ravi became ready for this marriage ceremony and accepted the proposal of the girl's family.

Ravi married Joanna. . The marriage ceremony was completed well. Ravi became a fan of the beauty of Joanna. His brother abhi was also there in the marriage ceremony but he went back to Punjab for duty the next day after the marriage ceremony so Joana did not meet him. 6 months of marriage ceremony was completed.

Now it was Ravi's turn to move to Punjab and perform his duty in that factory and Abhi was supposed to come back to Dhanbad. Ravi told his wife Joanna that is going to Punjab and he will come back after a few months. Joana said that she will also go but somehow Joanna agreed to be at home. Ravi said that he will come as soon as possible. Ravi was going to Punjab, so Joana was upset. When Ravi reached Punjab , Abhi came back to home in Dhanbad. Joana thought that Ravi had come back very soon. She asked how did you come so fast. Abhi gave a pleasant smile only and didn't say anything. As it was told earlier that Abhi and Ravi were twins. Joanna didn't identify that he is Abhi not Ravi. She started enjoying her married life with Abhi also. Earlier she was enjoying with Ravi but now she was enjoying with Abhi. She was unable to identify them. Abhi and Ravi continued this suspense for 2 years.

After completion of 2 years when Abhi was there at home Ravi also reached there because the factory of Punjab was closed. Now Abhi and Ravi both were present at home in front of Joanna. She was surprised and shocked to see them together. She was not able to identify who her original husband was. She understood that they were twins, so she asked who her original husband was. Ravi and Abhi both of them told her that both of them are her husband. She started crying and she asked if both of you had betrayed me. Please let me know who my husband is. Again the reply was the same, both were her husband. She was not willing to accept it. She was not willing to be the wife of two persons together. She told them that she wanted to go back to her parents' home. Then Ravi counselled her and said - don't worry, only one of us will be there with you, another will be always outside the state for earning. But she was not agree because she was not willing to continue with two husbands but there was no option. Ravi also said both of us will give our all the earning amount to you only because you are the only wife for both of us and our son and daughter will be nourished well and we can educate them nicely if earning is double. Pleas hue think about your children, not about yourself only.

Joanna said there is no option you have left for me. Already both of you have enjoyed my modesty, which was totally illegal. I cannot move to court for this because already I have lost everything which the court will never return and I also do not want to leave my original husband. Since there is no option so unwillingly I am there with you always.

Ravi and Abhi continue their life with one wife only. Joanna also accepted them and continued her life with both of them. All their villagers know these things but they never interrupted their life. They are living happily now.

****

27. She Sold Herself

This is the story of a young lady named Jessica. She was a beautiful girl . She was approx 20 years old and she belonged to a poor family. She got married to a person who was approx 20 years older than her. Her husband was a rich person. Her life was going smoothly. She was enjoying her life. everything required was available at her house. She was enjoying her married life. For a few years she was at home because newly married girls were not allowed to go outside the home. It was a trend prevalent in her society. If she wanted to go outside for shopping or entertainment she was going with her husband only.

Every neighbour was praising her beauty. She was happy and satisfied with her husband.

After a few years her husband became sick because of his old age and he was not having enough strength to do all the household work.

Jessica's husband was weak now and Jessica was very young and energetic. She was not very happy with her husband now because of his old age. Jessica was not having any children from her husband.

She got in an affair with a young boy named John who was living behind her house. Jessica and John both of them fall in love. Jessica started meeting with John every night on her rooftop and started enjoying intercourse with John. For a few months both of them enjoyed it a lot.

Now Jessica has become a second hand wife.

After a year John told Jessica that he wants to discontinue because he is tired of these things and is not able to enjoy every night with her. Jessica requests John that whatever he needs she will give him to continue with her and starts giving some amount every night to John. This is the first time I heard that a lady who was in love and surrendering herself for intercourse to her lover every night was giving lots of money also to her lover for this. For a few years it continued but after that John said that he is going out of station for higher study purposes.

Jessica has become very sad today. She made lots of requests to John not to leave her. But John denied and Jessica said okay but you can ask any of your good friends to enjoy with me and I will give money to him also for this but he should be very faithful.

John said okay I will ask someone. Next day John brought his friend Bunty and Raja with him. John introduced Bunty and Raja to Jessica and told Jessica that they are ready for that. Jessica denied she said why two people, only one was told. John said one was not ready alone, he was scared so both of them came together. Jessica gave her phone number and told to come at night when she will make a call. Now bunty and Raja together started coming every night to Jessica all were happy for this misdeed. One day I also got this offer of enjoyment but I completely denied it and I don't know for how many years and with how many youths Jessica continued this. I was transferred to a new city..

****

28. Accident

This is the story of Allahabad. There was a beautiful girl named Amisha in a middle class family. Her father was a government employee. Her brother was a college going student. Amisha was also a college going student. She was going to a girls college. she was studying for graduation. Her mother was a housewife. It was a very happy family.

Amisha's father was looking for a groom for her because she was able to be married. He told all his relatives to find a suitable match for Amisha. After lots of searching her father got a nice person for her. He went to meet him at his house. He was a gentleman working in the private sector. Amisha's father became very happy after meeting him and he fixed her marriage with that gentleman. The date of marriage came very close. All the arrangements were done properly. Her father was not willing to give any chance of a complaint to his new relative in the marriage ceremony. The day came and Amisha got married to that gentleman. She went to in-laws' house, and she was happy over there. Her husband's family also liked very much. The newly married couple were enjoying their married life. During the day our everyday her husband was going for the job by a local train to the nearby city.

After two years one day when he was going to catch the train for the job, he slipped and fell down and met with an accident. All those people who saw him, they took him immediately to the doctor but he did not survive. He was no more. God knows why it has done so. Amisha and her both the family cried a lot. Amisha was depressed. After a few days when everything became normal then also Amisha was not talking to anyone. Thank god she was not having any child.

Amisha's father and father in law both fixed a meeting and sat together for discussion about Amisha's future.

After one year both of them agreed for the remarriage of Amisha. They started looking for a suitable match who can be ready for the remarriage of Amisha with him. A day came when a nice person became ready to be married to Amisha. She was not willing to be remarried but under the family pressure and telling her about her future after the death of her parents, she agreed.

They fixed her remarriage ceremony. The day of the marriage ceremony came and Amisha got married to him. Thanks and salute to her second husband that in spite of knowing all these things he accepted her and agreed for the marriage. Amisha is now happy in her new life she is having two children.

****

29. The Dream came True

This is the story of Richa. She is a beautiful girl. She was in love with Ramu. But it was only one sided love. She met him only once in a marriage ceremony. Both of them were teenagers. After that she started liking him but she was not able to tell. They were distant relatives. She was back home. After a few years both of them meet again in a marriage ceremony. This time Richa disclosed her feelings to Ramu. She told him that she likes him. Recha's brother was a rowdy person. He has beaten many people in his village. Richa was scared of his anger. When Richa was disclosing har feelings to Ramu, he asked - what happened to you are you okay

See replied yes I am ok but I have liked you for many years and once I have seen you in my dreams that you have done everything with me. After that dream I started to like you more. Please accept my love. Please don't deny. Then Ramu asked - What about your brother, he is a very angry man. If he knew about us then he would hit both of us. She told you are right, but how come he will know the matter. He is not present here and we are not going to tell anything to anyone. And he is also a characterless person. He had intercourse with his cousin and one more girl that I know very well.

Ramu said okay what do you want with me. She replied I want you to love me. He said okay next time. In the evening Ramu was alone on his third floor then Richa came there and hugged him tightly. After that on the started kissing each other and did something more. They did everything with each other in love except intercourse. Richa said today my dream has come true. She had intercourse with someone else also earlier she discussed this by herself. After two three days she went back home and very soon she got married to someone. It was an arranged marriage by her parents. She became a second hand wife for him but no one knew about this matter. Now she is having two children and has become a rich lady. she is very happy in her life.

****

30. Miss Beauty.

This is the story of a servant Gangu. He was very good at household work. He was working for a reputed and well off family. The head of the family was a Police officer having many bodyguards. His youngest son also became a police officer.

In that family total nine members were there including Gangu. His owner was a powerful person. It was a very tough task to cook food both times for all 9 members in the family including tea, breakfast etc. All the time he was busy giving service to that family. That family had three cows. The service of cows was also his responsibility. when he was free we were gossiping with him sometimes.

Gangu was only eighteen years old. He was very strong and able to do all these works. In that family out of 9 members three daughters were there. All three daughters were very beautiful. One daughter was married and the other two were married.

The third daughter was the Miss beautiful of the colony. Many youths were deprived of having Miss Beauty as their girlfriend. But she was not able to have an affair with anyone because all the time her brothers and Gangu were safe guarding her. Some of the boys told me to pass their love letter to her as a messenger because I was a child so no one can doubt on me. But I denied.

God made her when he was totally free. She was having all the ability to be Miss India but her father did not allow it. So she became Miss Beauty of the colony only. I have seen her. She was as beautiful as a fairy. Second daughter of that family also got married now Miss Beauty was the one left

for marriage. but she was supposed to wait for 2 years for marriage and she was deprived of having a boyfriend, which was not possible so she wanted to have an affair with Gangu. She proposed to him. He was very lucky. He was going to have Miss Beauty as his girlfriend. Gangu was waiting for this proposal for years. Immediately Gangu hugged her and disclosed his feelings towards Miss Beauty. They loved each other for many years. They enjoyed intercourse also. One day Gangu
put a proposal of marriage in front of Miss Beauty. She scolded him badly and told - don't be a fool. You have enjoyed everything with me. Now, don't ask for marriage. You know my family better than me. If they come to know anything about our affair then they will hang you at the same time. Gangu said okay, I will never ask for marriage sorry. Next year Miss Beauty became married to a police officer. She became a second hand wife but no one knew it. Gangu cried a lot in her marriage. The family was thinking that he was crying for his sister's departure. But the matter was something else. After a few months he left that house forever and never came back.

****

31. Love in the village

This is the story of a village. All the villagers were living there happily. People of different caste and creed were living there. They all were enjoying their work of farming and other things. A person named Jugal was also living there. He was a very poor but very honest person. He used to help other families. He was a priest so he was going to meet all the families in the village whenever it was required. In the same village a person named Anant Singh was living here. He was a reputed and powerful person. He was father of three children, one son and two daughters. His elder daughter's name was Pallavi. She was a very beautiful girl. She was in her teenage years. He wanted to have a boyfriend but in the village it was not possible. She was deprived of a boyfriend. So made friendship with Ashok. He was living after a few houses from Pallavi. They were knowing each other earlier also because in the village every family knows each other but they were not having friendship. Ashok accepted her friendship and started meeting outside the village in a nearby market. But they were not gossiping a lot because villages were also present in the market and they could complain about it to Pallavi's father. Both of them fell in love with each other. Pallavi proposed to him and he accepted her proposal.

One day Pallavi planned to run away from the village. Because they were not getting enough time for love. Ashok said we are not having any job and any money so where we will go and how we will live.. Pallavi sad don't worry for money I will bring all the money and jewellery from my house you will arrange a rented house in the nearby City for living. Ashok said okay. He rented a house in the nearby City. He said Pallavi that I have taken a one bedroom set on rent. Tomorrow I will go with my cycle there and you will go to college after that we will move together to that house. Pallavi said okay this is a very good plan tomorrow we will implement this plan. Next day in the morning Pallavi went to college and she did not come back. Her parents became very worried and started looking for her everywhere in the village and all those areas near the college but they did not get her anywhere. All the villagers came to know these things. Pallavi's family was in deep distress. One day was over and Pallavi did not come back. Villagers are afraid of police so they did not lodge an FIR. Another reason was that they did not want to spread the matter because the family knew that if she had run away aur kidnapped in both the cases her family would be defaming everywhere. Villagers also corporate into these matters then never spread this kind of news to other villagers.

When pallavi's mother entered her room for brooming she became shocked after seeing that her jewellery was missing and the packet of the jewelry was thrown under the bed. She started crying and told it to her husband. He became very angry and thought that someone has stolen this. Same time Jugal came to meet him then he started beating him in panic and announced that he had stolen the jwellery from his house. The villagers told him- please don't hit Jugal. We can check his home if he has stolen there is no other place where he can hide it. Anant Singh agreed and went for checking is house but didn't get anything. He told him might have kept it somewhere else. Villages told - keep him in captivity but don't hit.   Anant Singh agreed.

Ashok was enjoying his life with Pallavi in the City. Family of Ashok came to know that he is also missing from the village. They understood that Pallavi had run away with Ashok only but they did not disclose this from anyone because Anant Singh was a powerful person and he can hit is whole family badly. Pallavi's whole family, her other relatives also including some of the villagers, were looking for her into the nearby city all the time. On the third day of her disappearance the villagers caught them in the City when they were roaming together to buy something. The villages hit Ashok and informed Anant Singh that they have got his daughter. Anand Singh moved immediately to the city with his family and brought Pallavi back home. When Pallavi reached home her mother and father both started beating her and asked to narrate the whole story. Then she said that he has stolen some money and jewellery and ran away with Ashok because she loves him and wants to spend her whole life with him. They again started hitting her and locked in a room. They stopped her going to college. Anant Singh asked forgiveness from Jugal and sad sorry in front of all the villagers because he did not steal jewellery and money.

Within one year they fixed Pallavi's marriage and sent her to in-law's house. She was now a second hand wife. But her in - law's family never knew this story because villagers always protect their daughters. No one discussed the matter. She is happy in her married life.

****

32. Love in the Cropping fields

This is the story of a nice village. In that village maximum persons were involved in agriculture only. The village was full of greenery. During the winter season the cropping field was full of lentils and grams. We all like to eat green leaves of lentils and grams. All the families and especially children like to eat the leaves of these lentils.

This was the duty of the children to bring lentils and gram leaves at home for the family but it was not necessary it was their choice.

Two children Priya and Neeraj were playing near their house. Priya was five years older than Neeraj. Priya was in her teenage years. She was approx 15 years old and Neeraj was only ten years old. They were cousins. She was a teenager and she was feeling safe with Neeraj. She always behaved with Neeraj as a friend. At least one friend was there with her. Priya fell in love with Neeraj but she was not able to tell him that she liked him because she was older and Neeraj was her cousin and unaware about these things. Priya was an adolescent girl. she was having lots of query and different things in her mind.

One day Priya planned to go to the cropping field in the afternoon to bring lentils and gram leaves. She made a request to Neeraj to come along with her because she doesn't want to go to the cropping fields alone. Neeraj became ready to go with her. Both of them moved to the cropping fields very happily. It was afternoon no farmer was there in the cropping field. Both of them moved little far from the village and started plucking leaves of lentils and grams. Priya was very happy today she said to Neeraj - let's play a game. I will be your patient and you will be my doctor. I am going to be unconscious and you will become a doctor for me. when I become unconscious you will rub my lower abdominal part then I will become conscious.

Neeraj said OK but if you will not hit me. Priya said okay and they started playing the game. No one was there in the cropping field so they enjoyed this game many times. Both of them were experiencing a new kind of pleasure. Very soon Priya asked him to do some more treatment as intercourse. Neeraj was also enjoying it so he became ready and did the intercourse in the cropping field. After some time they came back home. On the way Priya warned him not to discuss these things with anyone else. Neeraj agreed. After this many times they enjoyed intercourse whenever they got a chance in loneliness.

In the village it is still in tradition that they married their daughters at an early age. Her parents fixed her marriage with someone and she got married at the age of eighteen years only. She became a second hand wife of someone.

Neeraj was 13 years old now. Neeraj was looking for someone for that kind of pleasure which he has enjoyed with Priya. His other cousin Meera came to live with him. She was eight years older than Neeraj. She used to play all the time with him. In the villages children do not study in general. One day when they were on the roof at night and discussing different things, Neeraj said that he had enjoyed intercourse with someone. Meera said you are making me fool, you do not know anything about this. Then he told the whole story of his enjoyment from starting to last. Meera asked, "Do you want to enjoy it with me?" He said ok if you are interested. She said okay you can start but you are a child and I want to see your power and both of them enjoy the intercourse. Meera said you are only a kid for me and I am enjoying this thing with you just like a game. But ok you can continue playing the game and enjoy.

After this they continued it for years. Meera was going to be married. Her father has fixed marriage for her. She got married and became a second hand wife. After some time she gave birth to two children. She is very happy in her life. Priya became mother of three children and she is also very happy with her husband.

****

33. Boyfriends

This is the story of a very beautiful girl Shabnam **of** Edinland. In her childhood , she was a very cute baby. She was studying in the same school where one of my relatives was also studying. They were in the same class. They took admission in a college in a nearby City. Every day she was going to college by a local train. My relative was also going to the same college with her every day in the same train.

I have also traveled on that local train many times, the journey was so nice and pleasant. Every time when I traveled through that train I felt a new enjoyment during the journey. The train passes through the lush greenery and it gives the feeling of a dense jungle. If the train stops in between you will not find any way or any mode of transport to move from there except walking on foot, But thank God it never happened. The duration of the journey was one and a half hours.

One day when Shabnam was going to the college like every day by the train a smart student was attracted towards her. He was also studying in the same college and living in the same city where Shabnam was living. His name was Monu. They started talking with each other and slowly came together. Both of them fall in love. Shabnam was and open minded girl so she was discussing everything with Monu. They started moving together, eating together and sometimes dating also.

Shabnam's father was an army officer so different junior army persons were always visiting his home. One day a newly joined army person came to meet her father due to some official work. He saw Shabnam and liked her at first sight. For a few days whenever he was coming to her house started looking at her. Shabnam observed this and she also started liking him. He was a smart young dynamic and job holder person. Both of them started talking on different matters and very soon they fell in love with each other. Her father also observed this and asked about the matter from Shabnam. She felt ashamed discussing her affair. But she told her father that she likes him and he also likes her. Same thing her father asked from a junior officer. He also agreed on the same. They started dating and roaming here and there with each other. Shabnam's father observed this and fixed their marriage ceremony. Ring ceremony was done where all the neighbours and friends were invited. Both of them were ready for marriage. Few days back before the marriage, army personnel saw Shabnam when she was talking with Monu. He asked Shabnam about him then Shabnam told that he is only a friend and a classmate in the college, nothing else. But he didn't show faith in her statement and started spying on her. He came to know that earlier Monu was her boyfriend. Her marriage ceremony was in full preparation. Invitation cards were distributed to all the relatives and friends. The Mehndi ceremony has finished. Some of the relatives also visited her house. There were only three days left for the marriage ceremony. A hot argument between some and that army personal took place and he broke the relationship with Shabnam. That army personnel came to meet Shabnam's father and told that he is not interested for the marriage ceremony because of some avoidable reasons. Her father started shouting at him then he told that Shabnam is the main reason and she knows everything better he will ask his daughter first and he left their house forever and did not come back.

The marriage ceremony was stopped and all the relatives went back. Shabnam's father was very upset but she was not. She told her father that its very good that he broke the marriage beforehand. If he had not broken the marriage today, then their life would be hell after the marriage. They would never be happy in the relationship. And it was the matter of their whole life so God has done good for them. But her whole family was upset for a few days.

But Shabnam was not worried too much for this. Her father and brother started looking for a new groom for her and they found a suitable match in Pune. They fixed her marriage ceremony with his new boy in Pune. All the arrangements were done and the marriage ceremony took place at a given time. This time everything happened nicely without any disturbance. Shabnam got married with him and moved to in-laws house in Pune.

Shabnam was an open minded and a Frank girl. She did not want to live in a joint family because of lots of work pressure. Many times she argues with her husband for this. Her husband clearly said that he will live with his old age parents and he cannot live separately with his wife. But Shabnam was not ready to understand this. She did not want to continue the relationship in this situation and she fought with her husband after that she returned back to her home. She told everything to her parents and brother. Her brother was a rowdy person. He agreed with the subnams' decision. He moved to Pune and brought back all those items which Shabnam's parents had gifted in her marriage ceremony. Shabnam and her brother both moved to court and filed divorce papers and took divorce from him.

Shabnam went into depression. Shabnam has stopped talking to her relatives and all the time she was upset. She was thinking all the time that - where is her fault?

Her first marriage was broken without any causes are second marriage has also broken. She stopped coming out of her house then One of her neighbors who was just two three years older than Shabnam whom she was calling mama came to know all these things. Shabnam had been playing every day in her childhood with that mama.

Mama Ji came to meet Shabnam. She met mamaji, discussed all her problems with him and started crying. Mama ji consoled her and sympathized with her a lot. He started coming to meet Shabnam every day twice. Shabnam started discussing her problems with him and came out of depression within a few days. She was happy with him. Their meeting turned into an affair and they continued it for a few months. After one year both of them became ready for the marriage ceremony. They discussed it with their parents and after some hesitations their parents also became ready for this. Shabnam was married again. She became the second hand wife of mamaji. But mama ji didn't think about it. Thanks to him because he not only took Shabnam out of depression but also chose her as a life partner. Both of them are happy now and they are living abroad happily.

****

34. The Selfish Girl

This is a story of that time when I joined my office. There was a colleague she also joined along with me in the same office. Her name was Sanjana. She was a young, dynamic, talented , qualified and very beautiful lady. She was very very clever also. Every staff member was attracted to her . Every male member was willing to see her as his girlfriend. She was very Frank and she knew all these things. She was also playing well with everyone's emotions. She was very energetic and healthy. Whenever she was having one hour of free time or more than this she would jump over the wall of our office campus and go to her home and take a rest, because her home was just after a few buildings of our office. During lunch hours she was going to take lunch at home by jumping over the wall of the campus. We did not know about this. One day one of her colleagues saw her and complained to the boss.

Our boss called her and enquired and then she was completely denied and told that it is totally wrong she has not done this. After a few days she resigned from the job. Her fast friends asked her about this, then she said she has got a better opportunity somewhere as resigned and joined another organization.

There she made two boyfriends. One was in the same office , he was for office hours only and another was a Navy personnel he was for after the office hours of Sanjana.

She was enjoying all the free time after office hours with that Navy personnel. Enjoying evening hours in the park or dating in the restaurant and everything she was doing with that Navy person. He thought that she was completely made for him only. One day he gave a proposal of marriage to Sanjana then she completely denied. He became very upset and for a few days he was begging for marriage to Sanjana. But she clearly said she is not interested in the marriage ceremony with him and broke the relationship with him. He did suicide.

Sanjana came to know about this and she became upset for two three days after that she was normal. She said that such a sentimental person should not be her husband who can suicide for a girl..

Few years later Sanjana married someone else. It was an arranged marriage.

****

35. The Hotel Party

I was in Delhi working in a 5 star hotel. It was my first job after doing hotel management from a New Delhi based institute. Every day I was going on duty at 11 o'clock in the morning and coming back at 12 o'clock midnight. This is the story of all the mega cities. wherever I have visited I saw the same kind of incident in all the megacities. At midnight , I was coming back from the hotel to my home, then at the bus stop I was waiting for an auto because after midnight buses are not available and you will get an auto from the bus stand itself. A young girl with a boy was standing there and waiting for someone. A maruti car stopped in front of them. The girl started talking to them and the car owner gave her some currency. The girl took their currency and gave it to the boy who was there with her. After that the girl try to run away, then the car owner held her tightly until she became ready to sit in the car. Immediately that boy came back with the money he returned this currency then they freed the girl. You all can now understand in a better way what happened and why happened?

On the same bus stop everyday at night some of the young and adult girls were selling themselves to different people.

I took an auto and came back to my home.

Next day when I reached my hotel for duty I saw that in my duty chart they gave me duty in the lawn and party hall because there was a grand party at night. I started working for the party with some of my colleagues. Some of the outdoor catering members were also called for hard work. My boss was also there for the midnight party. The party started at 9:00 p.m. onwards. The people started coming one by one with their wives and girlfriends and they were enjoying snacks and hard drinks. The main party started at midnight. Loud music, DJ party, many dance floors, everything was there in that party. After midnight during the party and music they dropped their car keys into a box. All the people were supposed to take out one of the car keys from the box. The lottery system started for changing their wives. Who so ever had taken out a key, the wife of that car owner went to that person who got the car keys now. It was a lottery system for exchanging wives. One by one all the wives were exchanged this way. The original party started now. They all were enjoying it with each other's wives. The party continued till 4 o'clock in the morning. After that they all started going back with their own wife and the party was over. Thank God they did not cross the border line with each other's wife. But some of the hotels are there, where they do everything with other's wives after exchanging and they all enjoy doing it.

We were also backing home from the party. Next day again I was supposed to report on duty at the same time.

After a few months I resigned from the duty and never joined any other hotel because of their working hours.

****

36. The Dirty Uncle

This is the story of an adolescent girl Aditi. Her father was posted in another state and she was residing with her mother and brother under guidance of her uncle in a joint family. Her father was coming to meet them only once or twice a year. He was sending money for their survival and education every month on time.

Aditi was a teenage girl she was looking for a boyfriend all the time and she tried to made affair with many boys but she didn't success because those boys wear also teenage they were not showing maturity. They tried to have intercourse with her so she did not allow them and left all of them. She was deprived of a mature boyfriend which she did not get.

One day a smart boy named Mohit came to live in her neighbourhood. She liked him and he also liked her. Both of them started talking with each other and fell in love.

Aditi's uncle was going to Indore. He told every family member that is going to Indore for some business purposes. Aditi has never visited any place outside her village so she became rigid that she will also go with him.

He completely denied and said that - you are a young girl so where you will go with me I will be busy in my business meetings all the time. Aditi said - I will be there in the hotel and whenever you are free I will enjoy the tourism of that city with you. He refused but Aditi was crying so her mother made a request to her uncle to take Aditi also on tour. He said you can come with me.

Aditi became happy and full of joy she hugged her uncle and said thank you. Aditi packed her bag and became ready to move with uncle. Both of them left for Indore. They reached Indore and checked in the booked hotel. Aditi was full of joy because first time on tour. It seems that she has got a gold mine of joy. She was totally surprised that she had visited another City on tour. She visited historical monuments, some parks and mega marts. She was shopping in the evening for herself and her mother. Every day she was enjoying lunch and dinner in a star hotel. It was an unbelievable dream come true for her..They were there in the hotel for three days together in a twin bedroom.

After three days she boarded her train with her uncle and came back to the village. She reached her village, hug her mother and said thank you for allowing her for the tour. She was lost for the next three days in happiness. All the time she was discussing her tour only with everyone.

After three days she met Mohit. She also discussed the tour to Mohit. All the time she was discussing her tour only. Then Mohit said what's new in this. Many times I have visited Delhi for some work and enjoyed lots of tourism. Aditi asks about Delhi tourism. Mohit describes a lot. Aditi makes a request to him to take her also to Delhi next time. He said it is not possible, your parents will never allow you to go with any stranger anywhere. It will be better if you'll go with your uncle only. Aditi said okay I will ask my uncle to tour to Delhi but you will also come with me. Mohit said OK I will come in the same train and I will stay there in the same hotel where you will but I will not come with you so that your uncle should not know about our affair. Aditi said it's okay no problem.

After a few months Aditi started making a request to her uncle for Delhi tourism. Her uncle denied and said that without any purpose I will not go to Delhi. It needs lots of expenditures. Please wait whenever I will have my business meeting in Delhi. I will take you with me on tour. Aditi became fully obedient for her uncle; she was doing all his work on a single request. Her uncle told - I know why you are doing all the work. But I am happy with you so whenever I have a meeting in Delhi you must go with me. Aditi was very happy after listening to this.

After five months her uncle was invited for a business meeting in Delhi. he told it to Aditi, she jumped on her uncle and hugged him. Her uncle said - go and take permission from your mother then only you can go with me because I have to book tickets. She asked her mother and begged for her permission. Her mother allowed her in affection due to her madness for the Delhi tour. Aditi confirms to her uncle that she will also go to Delhi with him. He booked train tickets and a hotel room and told Aditi about this.

Aditi was full of joy. In the evening she met Mohit and told him about train tickets and hotel booking. She made a request to Mohit to book a room in the same hotel. Mohit agreed and booked a room in the same hotel. He took tickets for the same train. Aditi was very happy because this time her boyfriend will also be there with her. They plan a lot for Delhi tourism.

Date of Delhi to was very close. Aditi's uncle told her to pack her bag for the Delhi tour. Aditi was all time ready. On the scheduled date Aditi left for Delhi with her uncle by train. This time Aditi was more happy because her boyfriend Mohit was also there in the same train in another coach. They reached Delhi, checked into the hotel and took a rest. Her uncle told that he is going for a business meeting. She will stay in the hotel and order for lunch whatever she wants to eat. As soon as her uncle left the hotel, she moved to Mohit's room because he was there in the same hotel and he had told his room number to Aditi also earlier. They enjoyed their love life. They took lunch together and moved to a nearby park. She was in the laps of her boyfriend. Her dreams had come true. Before uncle's arrival she came back to her room. In the evening she was shopping with her uncle in different markets and mega marts in Delhi.

Every day the same routine was being followed and Aditi was enjoying her life with a boyfriend in his room and in the park. Last day her uncle booked a Delhi tourism bus and visited all the monuments of Delhi with Aditi. Next day they came back to the village by train. Aditi came back to her mother. Her dreams came true. It was her golden period.

Her elder brother was also there in the village. He knew all these things. But he did not know about Aditi's nature and her fraud.. He asked his mother - why did not his uncle take him also for the Delhi tourism. His mother said because you did not request, all the time you were busy with your village friends ,next time you will go.

Later on when he became mature he blamed his uncle for sleeping with Aditi. He made an allegation that in a hotel bedroom uncle has done wrong with Aditi. It was not only an allegation there was reality also because he was not expanding a single penny on her brother. His uncle said from the next time I will never go with Aditi. But Aditi's brother was trying to find out a cause to hit his uncle for this, and in a family dispute he hit his uncle badly. The reason was Aditi and became satisfied after hitting. Uncle was crying a lot because his nephew hit him today.

After a few years Aditi married someone. It was arranged marriage by parental choice. She was a second hand wife which no one came to know except Aditi They are happy in their married life. They have one son and one daughter. Aditi started flirting with her husband's friend. She also started flirting with her husband's Boss. She continued flirting with many people.

****

37. The Clever Girl

Rabiya was a very beautiful girl. She completed her schooling from a girls school and took admission in a lady college. It was a matter of discussion in her college that our parents have admitted as in a lady college so how will we get a boyfriend. A boyfriend is very very important for each girl in college life. Some of the girls suggested that the better boyfriend will be your cousins or those persons who are visiting your home frequently and faithful to your parents. So that you can meet them so often and your parents will not doubt you. Even if you want to go outside alone for some work, they will help you a lot.

Rabia was listening to all these discussions very carefully. She was also not having any boyfriend but willing to have someone. She started looking for someone as a boyfriend. She liked her brother's friend named Rishi who was coming to her home to meet her brother. He was a nice and brilliant student. Her parents also liked him. Rabia started looking at him. Rishi observed this and he was also willing to have friendship with her. One day when Rabiya's brother was not there at home and Rishi came to meet him . Rabiya went to talk to Rishi and offered her friendship to him by giving friendship card. Rishi accepted it and became very happy. Soon they started meeting and dating each other at home only on the roof. it was not possible to meet outside in that locality because everyone in the neighbourhood knew them. One day Rishi and Rabia both planned to run away from their house. Next day they ran away. Parents became very worried. Whole colony came to know that Rabiya had run away. Then her parents lodged an FIR of kidnapping against an unknown person.

They searched everywhere but didn't get their daughter. For three days enjoyed her life with Rishi and after that came back her home by herself by a reserve auto. As soon as the auto stopped near her home Rabia came out of the auto and fell down on the road and became unconscious.

Rabiya's mother started crying loudly that someone has kidnapped her daughter and she managed to run away from their captivity and became unconscious due to the kidnappers' fear and three days of hunger. They took her inside the home, poured some water on her face and called a doctor. But she became conscious before the doctor reached. The doctor came and checked and told them not to worry. She is well now. She was unconscious due to fear and hunger. Everything is ok now.

The police officers visited her home because they had lodged an FIR. They asked Rabia about har kidnapping then she told she has not seen anyone because they have given anesthesia and she became unconscious. When she became conscious she found her on the railway station and she ran away towards her home by an auto. Her parents took the FIR back because Rabia said that she did not know any of the kidnappers.

It was totally a fake story in front of police.

Next year Rabia got married to someone. She was now a second hand wife. She opened a medical shop and became owner of that shop. One year after her marriage she gave birth to a boy. During COVID she died of corona.

****

38. A Night in Calcutta

This is the story of Calcutta, West Bengal. One of my relatives named Aysha was working in a multinational company as a BPO. She was living in a one bedroom set with her friend Razia. She was also working in the same company. Both of them were going for duty together and coming back together in the company's cab. Razia was having many boyfriends.

The company was open for five days only in a week. Both of them were not on duty every Saturday and Sunday. They were totally free.

One day Razia asked Ayesha to enjoy the weekend. Ayesha said whatever you want to do you can do. I don't have any problem.

On Saturday night Razia invited her two boyfriends at her room for a party

Razia and Ayesha both were cooking non veg items for the party. The food was ready to eat. Razias' both the boyfriends came at 9:00 pm with a new girlfriend. They all started the party. They enjoyed non veg food along with some hard drinks. The party continued for three hours. At midnight they enjoyed themselves. Razia also enjoyed the midnight with them. After that they exchanged girlfriends and enjoyed themselves again.

At last they asked Ayesha for the intercourse but she denied and told please don't disturb I am going to sleep. They did not force her because they were already enjoying themselves with two girls. Razia also did not force her. They all left the flat in the morning and went back.

Next day Ayesha came back to her home. She was thanking all mighty God because she was safe from the midnight party.

She discussed all these things with her sisters. They suggested Ayesha live alone so she decided to change the flat. From Monday they reported for the job and within a week Ayesha rented a new flat for herself.

This is the culture in West Bengal that maximum girls are having boyfriends, and many of the girls have many boyfriends they use and throw each other after some time.

One day at 8:00 p.m. only I was roaming there near the Eden garden with my two friends.. Whatever I saw there it was totally surprising and shocking for me. The adult ladies were selling themselves to those persons who were interested in them for some amount. It was a new experience for me. I have never seen this kind of sale anywhere else. My friends suggested that we should leave the place immediately. Because dear pimps can be available for robbing. We left that place at the same time.

****

39. The Small hotels

This is the story of maximum small hotels of maximum cities. They indulge in many unfair means because it is their main earning. Some of the hotels are involved in flesh trade also.

One day one of my nearest friends came to my city for a business purpose and he made a call to meet me. I asked him where he was staying. He gave me the address of that guest house where he was staying. I went to meet him and I was totally surprised after seeing his guest house. I asked him that you are rich, why did you come to this very small guest house?"

He said because it was cheaper in rate than others. I did not understand his motive. Rooms were very small. No food and beverages facility was there in the hotel. Bathrooms were also dirty. I ignored all this things and continued gossiping with my friend. Lots of matters were there for our discussion. We were so busy talking that we forgot to see the time and it became 7:00 p.m. in the evening. I asked my friend to arrange some food because we were feeling hungry. My friend made a call to the manager and asked for some snacks. The manager denied and told me the messing facility is not available in this hotel because it is very small.

After 10 minutes the manager came to the room by himself and asked us -

Do you need a young lady?

I asked - for what?

He said for the enjoyment of your night.

I told him not required then he went back.

I told my friend - now I understand why you booked this small room in this small hotel. He was feeling ashamed in front of me.

After a few minutes I saw that approx twenty ladies were roaming with the manager in the hotel. He was applying one lady to each room wherever she was in demand.

I told my friend you can enjoy it. I want to leave because it is too late.

While returning back I saw that the manager was free and he was standing outside the hotel. I started gossiping with him in a friendly way then he told me that this is the main income for the hotel. I asked from where you bring this much ladies. He said that during the day they contact us and they give us the phone number so that I can call them for the customers. He also discussed with me that in the nearby villages where people are so poor their ladies come out at night to earn something with this and return back to their village in the early morning.

I came back but I was in sadness after listening to all these things.

****

40. Mr Idiot

This is the story of Mr Paul, a retired person. You can call him Mr idiot. Mr Paul was a government employee. He had a beautiful wife, one daughter and a son.

He was going to work every day. His family was a happy family but his wife was sick for a few years. Every day she was going for treatment to a government hospital. His Son and daughter were both adults.

They fixed the marriage ceremony of their daughter. An arranged marriage took place and their daughter got married to a person who was in a private job.. She moved to in-laws house but due to lots of work she came back after a few months and started living in her native home like earlier, most of the time she was living at home. She wasn't going to in -laws house due to fear of work pressure.

Her dear mother was more sick. In the beginning they helped her mother in going and coming back from hospital but when she continued they got tired of helping her mother and stopped helping her in her treatment. A time came when they all stopped helping their mother. She fixed an auto rickshaw and started going alone with the help of an auto driver.

Mr Paul was also not taking care of his wife. He was also tired of helping her. Mr Paul was retired and most of the time he was staying at home but in spite of that he was not taking care of his wife. He was getting a huge pension.

He fixed the marriage ceremony of his son Daniel. Daniel was an unemployed adult and did not agree for his marriage ceremony but under the family pressure he agreed and got married with a beautiful lady named Parul.

For a few months Daniel enjoyed his married life very well with Parul but after that when Parul started demanding some personal items for herself which was necessary, Daniel became upset because he was not having any money to fulfill the demands of his wife. Many times Parul asked for something like cosmetics, sanitary pads, toothbrush, shampoo, soap etc. and Daniel did not bring them because of the economic crisis. Daniel was an unemployed person and felt ashamed of asking money from his father because many times he had refused to give money to him. Daniel was getting tortured for these things from both the wife and father.

Mrs.Paul's one hand stopped working. She was very sick. Her daughter and son were also avoiding her then she moved to her village and never came back.

Mr Paul was a pensioner but the only earning person of his family. So he was behaving like a Hitler in the family. All the members were following his orders in the family. He asked his son to find a job in another state in different multinational companies. Daniel told how any company can recruit without any vacancy. Mr Paul became very angry and said - I cannot afford your and your wife's expenditures for whole life. So you have to find a job for yourself. Please move out of home and find a good job. Everyday his father was torturing him for the same thing.

Daniel made a request to all his friends to help him in getting a job in their company. One of his best friends was offered a job but it was in another state. Daniel became ready and told Parul that is going for a job in another state alone. Parul made a request to him to take her also along with him. She will cook food for him. Daniel said let me settle there firstly, when I get my salary I'll take a rented room then I'll call you there. Parul became ready but she was not happy, because there was no choice other than waiting for Daniel's call. Next day Daniel moved to another state, got a job there. Daniel was getting very less salary there. He sent a message to his wife that he is not getting enough salary so he is not able to call her there but after a few months he will call her.

Here Mr Paul was torturing Parul at home for very small things. He was having Parul at home just like a cat guarding the milk. Mr Paul's intention was not good for Parul. His wife was sick for many years, she was living in a room just like a dead body lying on the bed, so Mr Paul was willing to have an affair with Parul. He started catching her, overpowering her and kissing her for her very small necessary demands. Mr Paul started doing intercourse with Parul every night. In the beginning Parul fought with her father in law and shouted at him. Then Mr Paul said he will kick her out of the house if she will not cooperate. Parul has unwillingly accepted it because she did not have any place to go, Her husband was not there. Every member of the colony came to know about the relationship of Mr Paul with his daughter in law.

One day Daniel also came to know about the relationship and affair of his father and his wife. Then he cried a lot and never came back home. Parul was now a second hand wife of Daniel's father. Parul gave birth to a child. Mr Paul again became a father again in his old age. He was very happy. Parul was living with Mr Paul for many years so she also became very tight and now she started torturing Mr Paul. Because Mr Paul was in the age of seventy and Parul was in the age of thirty years so she was showing her power to Mr Parul all the time. But unfortunately she was living with him. Daniel never came back home and Parul's son is an adult now.

****

41. Struggle

This is the story of my childhood friend Patrick. He was a good student during his childhood. In the school we were together, in the college we were together. But after leaving college, he joined a non banking company because he was willing to earn on his own. He became very busy and rarely was we able to meet. It was very difficult to meet even once a month. We were supposed to make an appointment because he was very, very busy. Very soon we heard that he became a branch manager from the post of business progress office. After a year he became area manager. He was working well and earning well. It continued for 3 years. Suddenly I heard that his non-banking company has closed, because SEBI has stopped it and banned it all over India.. My friend who was earning well suddenly became unemployed. He had invested his own money and other neighbours' amounts also in the same non-banking company. Now neighbours' started asking for their money. Somehow he managed to return money of others and became free from the burden.

He was the eldest son out of four brothers and sisters. So his parents started putting pressure on him for his marriage ceremony.

But he completely denied it. One day one of his parents' relative's friends visited his home with his daughter to fix her marriage ceremony with someone in the same city where my friend Patrick was living. The opposite party denied the marriage to that girl because she was not highly educated.

Here Patrick's mother liked her as her daughter in law because she was so beautiful and excellent in household works. Patrick's mother liked it so much. She chose her as a daughter in law by heart. She discussed all this with Patrick's father. He said that if everyone is liking her then why would I deny and he also agreed.

Now it was turn for Patrick's approval. His parents called him in the room and discussed the same with him. Patrick knew everything and he had already seen her and became a fan of her beauty. Patrick said okay if my parents are ready then I am also ready.

The marriage ceremony has got fixed. That girl and her father moved to their village very happily and started preparing for the marriage ceremony.

Here in the Patrick's family all the arrangements have been made. Cards were printed and sent to all the relatives. They all visited his home. I was also invited as his best friend. I went there and attended his marriage ceremony.

I am also an artist so I made a painting on the topic of the band party of his marriage ceremony. The marriage ceremony was completed. His newly married boys started living with him. After a few days all the relatives were back home. One month has passed. Patrick's wife was also with him. His father started putting pressure on him for a job so that he can live his life in a better way. His mother and father both sar with him and asked him that - if your parents will not be alive after a few years then how will you manage bread and butter or both the times for you and your wife. So please leave your home and move somewhere to find a job. Patrick understood the matter well and said okay

I also want to do any kind of job but I don't know where to go for this. His father told move to Delhi and meet my friend Sachin Singh who is in a multinational company. He will help you a lot.

Next day Patrick packed his bag and moved to Delhi by train. He reached Delhi and met Mr. Sachin and discussed all these things. He told him that in my company there is no vacancy but there is a new company going to be started within a few days. You can get a job easily there and wherever you will need my help I am always ready.

Patrick became very happy that very soon he was going to get a new job in a multinational company. He applied for the job, passed the interview and got a job as a store incharge in that company.

Some staffs were also working under him. Into that company many female staffs were also there. Battery liked one of the staff named Pushpa. They introduced each other by themselves because they were in the same company. They started meeting so often. They started dating. Pushpa was so beautiful that anyone can like her. Pushpa was in love with Patrick. He was also in love with Pushpa in spite of being married to someone. She was also a married woman. Both of them started living together and they were enjoying their life.

After a few months when the managing director of the company saw Pushpa he called her into his cabin and offered her promotion. The managing director started liking her and soon he fell in love with her. Pushpa also started liking him and she also started avoiding Patrick. When Patrick came to know all these things he became very upset and resigned from the job from that company because he was not able to see his second wife into the laps of his managing director. He was depressed for one week. But slowly he came out of this trauma..

Patrick joined another company and his salary was little more here. He was a mad lover. He was looking for someone to fill the gap of Pushpa. After a few months one day he saw Roma in his company. Roma was a beautiful lady and mother of a child. Her husband was unemployed and a habitual permanent drinker. So Roma left him and came to Delhi and started doing a job in Patrick's company. Patrick did not know all these things so everyday he started meeting Roma with some of the excuses. Roma understood the matter but she didn't say anything. One day Patrick offered his proposal to Roma. She didn't say anything and accepted his proposal. Both of them started meeting in a restaurant. They also started dating each other. After the working hour they were not able to talk to each other so Patrick gave her a new cell phone. Now they were able to be in touch 24 x 7. They came into a relationship and maintained it for years. She was the unrecognized third wife but second hand wife for second hand Patrick. Both of them knew about each other but they agreed on the same.

The distance came between them when the original wife of Mr Patrick came to Delhi to leave with him. From the last 15 years Mr Patrick is living with his original wife in spite of that he has maintained his love affair also till date.

This is not the story of only one Patrick. Many such kinds of Patrick are present in our society.

****

42. The Petrol Pump Manager

This is the story of a petrol pump manager Mr Tony . He was a very good manager. He was going on duty on time and coming after completion of his work. He was very punctual on duty. But he was greedy also. Many times it happened that he prepared a false report and stole some amount. When he was stealing small amounts no one was able to trace him. One day he took out rupees 50000 and came back home. When the owner of the petrol pump Mr Graham came to know about the theft of rupees 50000, he did not lodge an FIR because he was mixing kerosene oil in the petrol with the help of his manager to get more profit. He was also giving less quantity of petrol to its customers with the help of his manager. So, he visited the petrol pump manager's house with his bodyguard and driver. Mr Graham started shouting on Tony's gate - bloody Bastard Tony come out I will punish you well today.

Tony was not coming out then his wife asked him- why are you not going to reply?

Someone is using abusive words for you then why are you silent here?

Tony replied yesterday I gave you rupees 50000 that belongs to Mr Graham. I have stolen it from his petrol pump. He is shouting at me for that only. So please go and deal with the matter and tell him that I am not at home unless he will kick me out of the job.

Tony's wife went out and said welcome Mr Graham - please come inside my house. Mr Tony is not here. I want to talk to you. Why are you using foul language outside without knowing the fact.

Mr Graham was in an angry mood. He said firstly send Tony outside. Then Mrs. Tony gave a pleasant smile and took Mr Graham inside her house. She offered him a glass of water and cold drink both. After seeing the pleasant smile of Tony's wife Mr Graham cooled down. But he told Mr Tony has taken rupees 50000 without my permission and any information to any staff so please ask him to return my money. Mrs Tony said OK please be cool. This is a very small amount for you. And you know that Mr Graham is helping you everywhere so please forgive him this time next time he will never do it again but I will request my husband that if he has taken you will return it to you.

Mr Graham was not pleased, he said this is not the first time that I will forgive him many times he has stolen small amounts that I have already forgiven. But this is a big amount so I will not forgive. I want to get it today itself.

Tony's wife said ok let me see. See went inside and talked to Tony about what to do? Tony said please protect me unless he will kick me out of the job.

Tony's wife came to Mr Graham she sat near him and told him, money is not at home. Please forgive me for this time and please tell me what I can do for forgiveness. Mr Graham thought that she would not return his money so he hugged her and kissed her. She was not cooperating and fought with him but did not shout. Mr Graham overpowered her and raped her. She told Mr Graham you have done very wrong with me. I will lodge an FIR against you. Mr Graham said OK Mr Tony will also move to jail with me and left her house.

Mrs Tony came back to her husband and slapped him and told you I have lost my modesty today because of you and you were sitting quietly inside the house. Tony used sympathized words, he told you are my wife and always I am there with you. I am very sorry that I did not save you because if I would be in jail you and our son and daughter would all be on footpaths. Please forgive me for this. Thank you for saving me. He accepted his second-hand wife willingly because of his own fault.

The matter did not stop here. After this episode many times Mr Tony has stolen money from the petrol pump and Mr Graham came to his house and had intercourse with Mr Tony's wife in lieu of his money. It became a routine affair for them on a monthly basis. All the neighbours of Mr Tony came to know this but no one was speaking in front of Mr Tony so he also did not care about it.

One day Mr Tony died in a road accident.

Matter was over.

****

43. The Sale

This is the story of Calcutta, I was there only for a few days. I saw many things there. I visited Victoria memorial and I saw that in the park openly girls and boys were everything except intercourse under the trees. God knows what kind of education the parents have given them. They were not worried about what people will say and think. They were busy enjoying each other. Being in love is different but displaying it to others is shamelessness. I observed that in mega Cities maximum family have 1 or 2 BHK flats due to lots of expenses and they do not give moral education and proper time to the children. Because of that the children are shameless.

In this modern era children have lots of their own expenses like visiting costly restaurants, lots of shopping, buying new clothes always to maintain their class, offering meals to the girlfriends etc. These expenses are unnecessary for us but it is very very important for them. And if parents are not giving this much amount to them they try to earn it through different modes generally illegal.

One day in the afternoon I was standing on a bus stop waiting for my bus then I saw that to very beautiful girls just like princess got down of an auto having very costly smart phones in their hand came there and started waiting for someone. A very big black car reached there. A boy came out of the car and started bargaining with those two princesses. The girls were asking for Rs 20000. The boy agreed on Rs.18000 and gave it in the hands of one of the girls. One girl sat into his car and the car moved very fast. The second girl who received the money took an auto and

moved. It was totally a flesh trade. The girls were selling themselves for money. The first girl had given money to second girl because money will be safe they cannot snatch it back after enjoyment. The beauty and the style of those girls were disclosing that they were from good families.
What will happen to that person who will be marrying with these girls?

****

44. Shamelessness

Few years back I visited a historical monument old fort in Delhi. Many new loving pairs were sitting under different plants and shrubs and disclosing their shamelessness to others. It was clearly visible that they were having hunger for sex. There love was not true it was totally fake only to full fill demands for each other. I saw something surprising and shocking there. A lady came with her approx 6 years old daughter. She sat under a tree. After a few minutes a male member came and joined her. She give a ball to her baby and told her to play somewhere else in the nearby area. The girl started playing nearby. The ladies started enjoying with that person. God knows She was a second hand wife or more. She was so shameless that she was Indulge in unfair means with that person in front of her baby. The baby was observing everything and she was not feeling comfortable after seeing her mother in others laps. Since, she was a baby, so she was unable to stop her mother.

Please think for a minute.

What kind of lesson that lady was giving to her daughter?

What kind of student is being prepared for the nation?

Her mind will be always in pain to understand why her mother has done it?

Students of this age never forget this kind of scene. It will never be deleted from her mind.

It will not her mistake if she will do something wrong after being a teenager. It will be counted as her mother's mistake.

****

45. A Love Marriage Family

This is the story of a family, Mr Lucas, whose maximum members have a love marriage. Lucas was an executive engineer and he was getting a very nice payment. His college friend Julia wanted to marry him. Lucas agreed because he was also in love with Julia for many years. The Family of Lucas was not ready for this because Julia was from a different community. Lucas' family completely denied the marriage in spite of knowing the fact that Lucas married Julia. Lucas' family forgot him forever and told him not to visit them.

Lucas started living with Julia where he was having his posting. They were living happily. They loved each other so much that Julia gave birth to five children one by one. Two sons and three daughters were there. For a few years they all enjoyed a happy life. They were very happy. The children were very happy.

But after 21 years at the time of marriage of the children they suffered with lots of problems.

The elder daughter Reema was in love with her boyfriend who was studying with her in college and wanted to marry him. All the time they were visible together. They enjoyed a lot of love in their college life. They were known as love birds. Whenever he was visiting her house, he was being treated as a very important guest.

Each and every member of the family was available in his service. One day when Reema's family gave him a proposal of marriage with Reema, from the next day he stopped coming to her house and denied the marriage.

Reema was crossing the age of her marriage so they put a proposal on a matrimonial site. A person who was working in a private company and looking smart also became ready for marriage with Reema. Her family did not investigate his family background or anything else and got ready for the marriage. The event took place and Reema got married to him. Very few people were present at the wedding and from the groom's side only five friends were there. After marriage when Reema reached her in-laws house, no one was there except her husband. It was a rented flat. She lived there
Only for a month after that both of them came back. Reema's family asked for the matter, and then her husband told that she is pregnant and since no one is there to serve her, she came here. All the family members can take care of her in a better way. Reema's family agreed with him. He went back and promised to come on a monthly basis. After a few months Reema gave birth to a boy. Whole family became very happy. The child was getting love and care of mother and fathers both at his maternal grandmother's house. It continued till 5 years after that his father stopped coming and didn't return. The child is an adult now and residing with his mother's family in my neighbourhood colony. The second child of Mr Lucas got a government job and married his girlfriend.

Mr Lucas got posting in another town. His third daughter Barbie fell in love with a neighbouring person Mr. Sanju. Barbie asked her parents to give a proposal of marriage to family of Sanju. Mr Lucas visited the house of Sanju and gave a proposal to his parents for the marriage of Sanju and

Barbie. They agreed with the proposal and Sanju got married to Barbie.

The fourth child of Mr Lucas' daughter Sonia got in an affair with the younger brother of Sanju. Her affair continued for 3 years. She did everything with him before marriage and got pregnant then her family arranged her marriage with him in a hurry.

The fifth child of Mr Lucas was Oliver. He was average in his studies. Most of the time he was busy with all the household work because service to the whole family was his duty. He saw a very beautiful girl in the market and fell in love with her. He asked me how he would propose to her. I suggested asking her name first. He asked her name and after that his love affair continued for three months.

One day Oliver was kidnapped for a few hours at gunpoint. His kidnapper was the ex boyfriend of the girl. He told Oliver that you have two options: either you will forget your love affair or I will kill you today itself. Oliver was not ready to forget his girlfriend. Kidnappers were willing to shoot him then a carpenter who had worked at Oliver's house saw all these things , appeared in front of them and somehow he managed to save Oliver's life after promising kidnappers that Oliver will forget his girlfriend forever. He told the whole matter to the parents of Oliver. They scolded him badly and told life is more important than a girlfriend so forget forever. We want the safety of our child first. Oliver forgot his girlfriend under this much pressure but he was very disheartened. He was very upset for a few months. He is around 50 years old and still unmarried.

****

46. The Judgement

This is the story of a government employee named Henry. He had a brilliant mind. He is tall but not very smart. After joining a job he got married with someone in his own community. It was an arranged marriage. His wife is very beautiful. Her name is Sujan. He was very happy in his life. After a month of the marriage his wife wanted to go back to her parents but Henry did not allow her because he wanted to spend some more time with her. Sujan said that she is pregnant and not able to do all the household work so she wants to go to her home so that the child should be healthy. Henry became happy and allowed her to go to her parents after listening to all these things. She went back to her home. Henry was going to meet her on a monthly basis to know her well being.

After a few months Sujan gave birth to a baby. The daughter was very beautiful. Henry was very happy because he became a father now. Henry asked her to come back to in -laws ' house then she completely denied it. She said that till the time the baby is small she will not go to in -laws house. Henry understood her problem; he also wanted the well-being of the baby. He started going to meet his wife and daughter so often. He was fulfilling all the demands of his wife. Henry wanted to live and spend more time with his baby. So after one year he pressured his wife to come to the in-laws house but she again refused. Henry asked his father in law to send Sujan with him then he replied he doesn't have any problem if Sujan agrees but he cannot force his daughter to leave the house.

Henry became unhappy because Sujan refused to come with him. He came back because he was supposed to go on duty every day. Three years passed but Sujan did not come to her in-laws' house. His baby is now 3 years old.

One day Henry went to meet Sujan and told that today anyhow you will come with me at my house unless our relationship will be over today itself because from the last 3 years you are giving lots of excuses on which I agreed. I am not going to listen to any excuses today. Either you will come with me or the relationship will be over. My daughter is 3 years old and she will start her schooling from my house. I want my baby's admission in a reputed nursery school. Sujan saw her husband's anger and she was not having any excuse today so she packed her bag and came back to in-laws' house with Henry.

Henry admitted his daughter to a nursery school. He was leaving his daughter up to school in the morning and in the afternoon Sujan was bringing her back. Henry was very happy with his small baby. He was disposing of all the responsibilities of father very well. It continued till one month only.

After a month, the elder brother in law of Sujan came to meet her. Sujan packed her bag and moved with him without giving any information to Henry. She told everyone in the in-laws house that her father is very sick so she's going to an emergency. Henry came back in the evening from the duty then he saw that his daughter and wife both were not there. He became very worried and asked his parents then they told that her father is very sick so she went back with her elder brother in law to her home to meet him.

Henry made a call to his father in law and asked about his health. He replied that he is fine. Henry asked - if you are well then why Sujan told in the house that you are very sick and she went to meet you with her elder brother in law. It means both of them were lying.

He replied I am very sorry for that, let her come. I'll ask about the matter.

Henry became very angry. Next day he moved to Sujan's house. He reached there and asked her -

Why did you come back without informing me?

Why did you and your relative both lie?

Sujan replied - because I was not feeling well in the in-laws house.

Henry said you are my wife you should come and go anywhere with me not with other relatives now back you back and come with me immediately.

Sujan refused to go with him.

Henry said - if you will not come with me then our relationship will be over today.

Sujan said as you like, but I will not go anywhere.

Henry came back in anger and stopped going to meet Sujan. Sometimes during the festivals he was going to meet his daughter only. Later on he came to know that Sujan was in a relationship with the elder brother in law and Sujan's family was aware of that. Now Henry was repenting on his marriage. He has got a second hand wife in spite of knowing the fact that he is ready to compromise but she doesn't want to live with him. He stopped giving money to his wife for all her expenses.

After a year Sujan lodged an FIR against Henry that he is not giving money for different kinds of necessary expenses and trying to divorce her without any causes. The matter moved to the court where Henry answered that he is always ready to live with his wife but she does not agree because she is in a relationship with the elder brother in law. Sujan replied this is not true. She doesn't want to live with him because she doesn't feel well in the in-laws house. The court ask Sujan to compromise and leave with Henry but she denied it.

The court said that the court make a request to Henry to give some amount every month for the nourishment of daughter only not. The court will not force Henry to give expenses to Sujan because she has denied living together. Henry is giving some amount every month for the needs of his daughter.

Their daughter is 13 years old today. She is suffering more than others. She did not get love from both of her parents together.

They are still fighting in the court.

Henry is asking for divorce but Sujan is not giving.

Sujan is asking for his half payment but Henry is not giving.

The court is puzzled with their case and asking them to compromise.

****

47. A Placement Agency

There was a placement agency in a mega city. This placement agency was unregistered and indulged in unfair means. When it was started it worked as a placement agency only for a few months after that they started a networking company named DVRU company. They open their branches in ten different cities of the state. They were in profit of millions of rupees. Thousands of unemployed ladies got stuck into their trap. The girls were told to make a call to wealthy people and to win the confidence and to transfer money in different accounts by telling them that they have won the lottery and they have to give some amount as token money to get the prize money transferred into their account. And they were sending some SMS links to them. As soon as the party was touching the link the money was transferred into the account of DVRU company's MD. He was using so many mobile phones and SIM cards for this purpose. They were using one sim card for one fraud only. When an FIR was lodged against them in many cities they started a new business.

They offered jobs to unmarried ladies only. This is the story of that time when COVID-19 was spreading everywhere and people were unemployed. They gave them greedy offers. They were told to give them office jobs and during the interview all the members molested those girls one by one. One day they were having an interview of one girl only and during molestation they were making video clips also. They gave them jobs in networking companies and whenever they needed them they molested them either by blackmailing or on the gun point. They pushed them to the flesh trade if they denied they were threatened by them to upload their video clip on the internet.

A girl tired of the blackmailing and went to the police station. She described the whole story of her molestation and lodged an FIR. She disclosed everything about the company to the police. When the matter came into light approx 80 FIRs were lodged against them in different cities by different girls and somewhere by the boys also. The MD has got married with many female employees in different cities and after getting bored of them he divorced them also. Police arrested maximum founding members of the company and sent them to jail but their MD flew away. The criminals formatted their cell phone before arrest and broke the sim card. The police are trying to collect all the data with the help of a cyber cell.

Unwillingly many of the girls got stuck in their trap and lost their…………and became second hand wives.

****

Blurbs

I lived in the village for a few years. After that I came back to a very famous City. From my childhood to till date whatever I have seen and observed to most of those things are there in my mind and whenever I am free I want to write about all those incidents.

This book which I have jolted down is the result of minute observation of all the events and incidents happening around me. All the stories given in this book are true to the best of my knowledge.

The main aim of writing this book for the public is to make all the people aware about some characters which are present in the society but invisible.

The culprits and victims of my different stories belong from both village areas and different mega cities. Some of the culprits are illiterate, uncultured and some of them are highly literate and highly cultured.

In some of the stories I have shown carelessness and unawareness and in some of the stories. I have also shown bad conduct of some of the people.

I could not change the life of all those who have already suffered, about whom I have written in the book but with the help of this book.

I want to pass a message to all the people to protect their children and themselves.

Thank you.

www.ingramcontent.com/pod-product-compliance
Lightning Source LLC
LaVergne TN
LVHW041607070526
838199LV00052B/3023